Secrets of the Teachers' Lounge

Beverley Holden Johns

TRUTH BOOK PUBLISHERS

© 2014 by Beverley Holden Johns

ALL RIGHTS RESERVED. No part of this book may be reproduced or transmitted in any form or by any means, including but not limited to, electronic or mechanical, including photocopying, recording, or by any information storage and retrieval system without express written permission from the author.

ISBN: 978-1-940725-35-2

Truth Book Publishers
Franklin, IL 62638
www.truthbookpublishers.com
877-649-9092

Printed in the United States of America.

ACKNOWLEDGEMENTS

To Family and Friends who kept encouraging me to finish this book

To Marie Latzanich, who gave the book its title

To Marjory, Kathy, Paul, Herb, and Fran who gave me wonderful ideas to thicken the plot and rendered lots of positive support over several years

To Gene who taught me so much about fiction writing

To the Fort Lauderdale Writers Group who assisted me in the early stages of this book

Table of Contents

Chapter 1	1
Chapter 2	6
Chapter 3	13
Chapter 4	19
Chapter 5	26
Chapter 6	30
Chapter 7	35
Chapter 8	40
Chapter 9	44
Chapter 10	50
Chapter 11	55
Chapter 12	63
Chapter 13	69
Chapter 14	76
Chapter 15	81
Chapter 16	88
Chapter 17	93
Chapter 18	103
Chapter 19	112

Chapter 20	117
Chapter 21	123
Chapter 22	129
Chapter 23	134
Chapter 24	138
Chapter 25	143
Chapter 26	147
Chapter 27	151
Chapter 28	155
Chapter 29	159
Chapter 30	163
Chapter 31	167
Chapter 32	172
Chapter 33	177
Chapter 34	182
Chapter 35	187
Chapter 36	191
Chapter 37	195
Chapter 38	199
Chapter 39	203

CHAPTER 1

I will not allow this man to intimidate me. I know what I saw and I reported it to the Department of Children and Family Services. Wanda Terrill hit Jason in the face. I did the right thing. Thoughts and fears are rampant in my mind as I sit in the school office waiting area outside the principal's office.

It's now after school. All the students are gone and only a few teachers are still here. I have been called to the office.

I have that same feeling that one gets when waiting in the doctor's office for an appointment. My nerves are shot, my blood pressure is high, and I fear bad news that is coming. I know my face must be beet red. I look over my notes about the incident to keep myself busy. My mind wanders and I watch all around me.

Mrs. Depper, our school secretary, says smiling, "I'm sure Mr. Caton will be off the phone in a little while. Can you believe what that Mrs. Terrill actually did to Jason? I knew she was burned out of the job this year—too bad she didn't take a leave of absence. She just can't control her anger."

I smile knowing that I had better keep my mouth shut. I am already in enough trouble for reporting Mrs. Terrill for child abuse. I also don't know what Mrs. Depper may say to Mr. Caton.

Mrs. Depper figures out that I'm not responding, so she replies, "Well, I'm just the school secretary. What do I know about anything other than all this paperwork? I'm sick and tired of having to keep track of all this student activity money for Mr. Caton. It was never this difficult before to get accurate records of the money."

The phone rings. Mrs. Depper answers, "Lincoln School, how may I help you?" There is a long pause, "Yes sir, I will give him the message you called. I'm sure he'll call you back as soon as he gets out of his meeting."

When Mrs. Depper gets off the phone, she looks at me, "Well, seems like you have caused quite a stir. That was Mr. Clyde calling, and he wants to hear from Mr. Caton as soon as your meeting is over." Mr. Clyde is a school board member and his wife, Maybelle Clyde, teaches at our school.

Maybelle is a number one troublemaker in our school and is a good friend of Wanda Terrill. Oh, no, now I am in even more trouble. What have I done?

Out comes Mr. Caton from his closed-door office, scowl on his face, as he says, "Dana, come in here." I walk in his office and sit down in the closest chair. He closes the door. I am already feeling very uncomfortable. I am working hard to be calm and act in control of the situation.

Mr. Caton has been our principal for the last three years. I have never felt comfortable around him. I find him slimy; there is something about how he eyes all the women and how he seems like a fake with the students. I have been in the district 19 years. He is younger than I am. My fellow teachers and I guess he's about 35 years old. He is about 5 feet, 6 inches tall.

We joke all the time that he has a complex about his height and tries to intimidate everyone around him. He's not bad looking, but sure not my type with his domineering obnoxious personality.

Is it warm in this room? Am I having a hot flash or is it sweltering?

Caton starts in on me, "Now, Dana, what is this preposterous story that you saw Wanda Terrill hit Jason?

I'm sure there's some misunderstanding. I have known Mrs.Terrill since she has been here and you and I both know she would never do anything like that". What were you doing out of your classroom in the first place?" Mr. Caton is still standing; he is in front of me, looking down at me. Another intimidation tactic I recognize from him.

I say very calmly, although I feel like I could cry any minute, "I have my notes about what I saw and what I conveyed when I called the Department of Children and Family Services. I'm happy to review those with you."

Mr. Caton is getting red in the face. He gets loud and glares at me," Wait just a minute. What did you say? You called the Department of Children and Family Services and didn't tell me? How dare you not follow proper protocol in this school? You may be one of the senior teachers here but you will follow orders." If looks could kill, I would be dead.

I say in a matter of fact tone, "Mr. Caton, I am a mandated reporter. When I see an incident that involves abuse of a child, I'm required to report it, and that is what I did."

"You should have come to me right away before you made such a call," Mr. Caton bellows.

I talk fast, "Mr. Caton, I did come right to the office to report to you when it happened, and Mrs. Depper said you had left to go to a meeting and wouldn't be back until after school. When I told her I had to see you, she tried to reach you on your cell phone but there was no answer. I knew this couldn't wait so I called the Department and spoke to an investigator." By now, my hands are sweating and I feel like my face is on fire.

Mr. Caton's face looks like a red light. "Can you imagine how I felt when I got back to this office and had a message to call the Department of Children and Family

Services? Then, when I called them, I was told that an investigator will be here tomorrow morning. How dare you report something when you may not even know what you saw? How dare you go over my head? We should handle this inside our school building, within our family here, not going outside." Caton stretches his arms out.

He continues, "This is just absurd. Did you say you have written notes about this situation?"

"Yes, I do, and I've made you a copy for your records. Please do read it over and let me know if you have questions. I'm very upset about what I saw."

Mr. Caton takes the paper from me, gets an even worse look on his face, and sits down in his chair. At least he is no longer hanging over me.

I feel a little more relaxed but the feeling doesn't last long as he looks up from the paper and responds, "Now you have Mr. Bates involved in this? How did he see what was happening? It isn't any of his business—he's the janitor. If he would spend more time cleaning this building, we would all be a lot better off. I know you would agree with that statement, Dana. We all know that Mr. B. is getting old and doesn't clean well."

Mr. Caton is trying to get me off track. I don't take the bait, "Mr. B. did see what happened, and he also called Department of Children and Family Services right after I did. I had just taken my students to music, and was walking down the hall. I went by Mrs. Terrill's room. She was speaking loud to Jason."

I pause and continue, "She was yelling at him. The door was open to her classroom and I stopped to see what was going on. Mr. B. had been cleaning a spot off the hall carpet and heard the noise, and came down the hall. Mrs. Terrill didn't see us and kept screaming at Jason. Jason then called her a name, and she slapped him in the face. Both of us saw it."

Caton responds, "Well, sometimes our mind plays games with us. You may have thought you saw something, but you may not have really seen her slap him. You did say that he called her a name. Maybe she was just trying to get his attention. I'm sure there's a logical explanation."

Caton pauses and speaks in a very formal tone, "Miss Lawrence, you are free to go. I want you to think long and hard about your actions, and what you actually saw. I am sure Wanda can explain what happened. Did you even bother to ask her about what happened?"

I say in a firm voice, "No, Mr. Caton, I didn't ask her what happened." It's my job to report what I saw so someone else can investigate it. It isn't my job to investigate it myself."

Mr. Caton opens the door for me to leave, "I will see you in the morning, Miss Lawrence, that will be all."

I have definitely been dismissed. I'm shaken. I'm not sure what to do or where to go. I need to talk to someone. I head toward the teacher's lounge.

CHAPTER 2

The nerve of that man. He's a snake. I shake and fight back the tears while walking from the main office and away from the angering encounter with my principal. It seems eerily quiet with everyone gone. The custodian, Mr. Bates, is usually cleaning rooms but he's not around. The teachers' lounge is empty. Back in my room, I pick up my lesson plan book, twenty-six writing papers to grade; I put them in my teacher bag as I head toward the door of my classroom.

I get ready to turn off the light; I pause and look around my room. This is my home away from home, where comfort and solace are usually found. I look at the children's desks. I think about how those desks will be filled tomorrow morning by my eager 5th graders.

Yes, this is life's reward but why do there always have to be so many outside forces keeping me from doing my job. I have a principal who wants me to sweep under the rug the truth about the abuse of a child by another teacher, I know a teacher who would actually hit a child and another teacher who spends more time being a troublemaker than a teacher. I flip off the light. The whiff of the chalk dust and smelly sneakers is obvious; reminding me that Mr. Bates didn't get my room clean.

A quick glance in the teacher's lounge shows me someone has left part of a cake and a cherry pie out. I go in the lounge, grab some foil from the cabinet, cover them, and put them in the frig.

In the parking lot, there is only my car and the principal's. There's another car pulling out of the lot but it doesn't look familiar. It's white, but I'm not sure of the make of it. Maybe someone is just turning around.

People are always using our lot when the kids have gone home.

I get in my car, pull out my cellphone, and engage in my daily ritual of calling my mother every day on my way home from school. I try to be careful when I talk to her since she is 80 years old and still worries about me like I was 5. Mom answers.

"Mom, how was your day? Just wanted you to know I'm on my way home from school and am spending the evening grading papers."

"Dana, so glad you called. The talk of my bridge club today was the rape over on 17th street. That was terrible. Has Ashton said anything about it?"

Ashton is my boyfriend of two years and he is a lieutenant at the police department.

"I know he's been very busy, Mom, but don't know any of the particulars."

Mother continues, "Dana, you sound upset, is something bothering you?"

"Mom, I'm just tired. The kids were pretty wound up today. They are excited about Thanksgiving vacation, I guess. I just need to get home and go to bed early."

"Oh, okay, dear, you do sound tired. Are you sure there isn't anything else?"

I say, "Ashton isn't coming over tonight. He left me a text message that he was working on a case. Guess it's the case you're talking about."

Mother isn't convinced, "Are you sure you aren't coming down with something? I can come over with some soup for you."

"Thanks, mom, but I just want to get caught up on some grading."

"Well have a good evening and be sure to watch the six o clock local news. Maybe Ashton will be on about the rape."

I arrive at my condo. This is the place to shut the world out for a little bit. Duty tells me to call Reba, my best friend, and fellow teacher from school. In her text message, she had written, Call me right away. Too complicated to explain.

I drop my bag on the couch, and go to the refrigerator to grab a diet coke. Something a lot stronger is needed after the day I've had, but I'm not into solitary drinking. I dial Reba's cell phone. She answers right away, "Hi, Reba, just got in the door, what's up? Have I got loads to tell you."

"Oh, Dana, I didn't think you heard. Mr. Bates has been suspended until further notice. He had to leave right away. Mr. Bates was so upset that he came to my room. He didn't know what to do. I told him he'd better leave right away since Maybelle's husband is on the school board, and has the right to suspend him. "

I am shocked. "Oh no, I feel awful about this."

Reba continues, "Can you believe that Maybelle told her husband what happened, and got him to suspend Mr. Bates. I told Mr. Bates to call the district union president, Jessica, right away when he got home. I hung around awhile to see you when you got out of the meeting, but when everybody was leaving, I decided to get out also. What happened to you?"

I answer, "This is all my fault. Poor Mr. Bates, he will be lost without this job. We have to help him. I'm going to call him right away."

"Dana, you can try, but I already called to see if he got home okay and there isn't any answer. He doesn't have a cell phone. Tell me what happened in your meeting. I am dying to know. Troublemaker Maybelle was telling everybody you and Mr. Bates had made up terrible things about Wanda Terrill. I set them straight about what really happened. Are you okay? You weren't suspended, were you?"

I rehash the whole event and cringe while telling her the details of what that slimy Caton asked me to do, "Oh, Reba, Caton actually had the nerve to tell me I needed to recant my story. He said I probably didn't see her hit the student. Can you imagine? Like I would make that up. He stood over me trying to intimidate me. It was all I could do to keep from breaking down and crying, but I sat firm and told him I knew what I saw. That man is a creep."

Reba says, "What was your first clue? Sorry, Dana, I don't mean to joke after all you've been through."

I keep going, "Then while I was waiting to see him, our school secretary, made some statement about having trouble with him about the student activity fund. What's that all about?"

"How did you leave it with Caton?"

"I told him I definitely saw Wanda Terrill hit the student. He told me to think about it overnight. That man infuriates me. Who does he think he is? We have lived through 10 principals in the 15 years we've been at Lincoln, and we'll outlive him. The nerve. How do incompetents get promoted to administrators?"

Reba warns, "You know you should also be calling Jessica and meeting with her. She is our union representative. You are going to need to have the union's support in this mess."

I answer, "Already done. I called Jessica when I learned I was getting summoned to the office, but she wasn't available so I left her a text message." I'll keep trying to get Mr. B. I'll call you back when I reach him. What are you and Barry doing tonight?"

"Barry is working late and should be home around 7. We'll have dinner and probably watch Law and Order. Are you going out with Ashton?"

"No. Ashton's on a case tonight. I'm just going to hang out and grade papers. I still can't believe what Maybelle had her husband do, and what she told people about me. She stops at nothing. I'll call you when I reach Mr. B. Oh, watch the 6:00 news. My mother says there was a rape over on 17th Street."

Reba assures me, "Don't worry, Dana, I'm sure everything will work out okay."

"Thanks. See ya."

It sure helps to talk the situation out with Reba. She is my best friend. We've both seen each other through some tough times, and really like working in the same building.

I dial Mr. Bates. The phone rings and rings with no answer. Wonder where he could be. I heat up some soup in the microwave and sit down at my dining room table where I can see the TV. I hit the remote and get the 6:00 news. Sure enough, Mom was right. There has been a rape of a 17-year-old about 2 miles from school. The victim lived in one of the new apartment complexes in that area. The news commentator describes the area, "While the apartments are new, this neighborhood has had a high crime rate."

I wait to see if Ashton might be on camera but he isn't. The chief of police, Dustin Andres, is being interviewed and responds, "At this time, we are continuing our investigation but do not have a suspect. The victim was badly beaten as well as raped. It is unclear whether she knew her assailant." I think, no wonder Ashton is busy.

I dial Mr. Bates' number again. There is still no answer so I leave another message that it is urgent he call me.

I pull out my writing assignments to grade. That should divert my attention. Twenty-six of them have to be reviewed. While I correct them, my mind keeps going back to my encounter with Mr. Caton. My emotions find me getting angrier and angrier at that man.

After I finish the grading, I owe it to myself to spend some time reading. While engrossed in my book, the latest Janet Evanovich, the phone rings. It has to be Mr. Bates. I answer the phone. "Hi, Dana here."

The voice on the other end says, "Ms. Lawrence, this is Alfonse Nollwood."

I think, oh no, what is the school board president doing calling me? Maybelle's husband must have asked for my suspension from teaching. What will I do?

I answer, "Yes, sir. How are you this evening?" I await the words "You are being suspended from your job" to come.

"Miss Lawrence, Dana, I'm calling with some very bad news." Mr. Nollwood pauses, "Mr. Caton was found dead tonight in the teachers' lounge." We don't know what happened, but there will be an autopsy performed. Perhaps he died of a heart attack."

I gasp, "Oh no, this is terrible."

"We're so sorry. We're calling all the staff at the school before it is on the ten o clock news. School will be in session tomorrow and we'll have counselors available. The assistant superintendent for instruction, Mr. Thomas, will be acting as principal until such time as we hire a new principal. Again I'm sorry to break this news to you. Any questions that might be asked of you should be directed to the School Superintendent. Good night."

The words for any questions don't come from me as I am in a state of shock.

Mr. Nollwood hangs up. I'm shaking. Mr. Caton was just with me. He was in his office when I left. He's dead—what happened?

CHAPTER 3

I comment as we walk by the lounge on the way to our classrooms. "Reba, look, the lounge is taped off with yellow police tape. The cherry pie I put away before I left yesterday is out again."

Reba asks, "Oh, no, why is there police tape there? I know Mr. Caton was found there, but Mr. Nollwood said it was a heart attack. What's going on? Are you sure you put the pie away?" Reba looks at me doubtful like I just thought I put it away.

I respond, "Police tape means there was a death. It's usually done at all scenes of death, including accidents. After school, I'm calling Ashton to see whether he can tell me what's going on." Ashton is my boyfriend and works as a lieutenant at the police department.

Reba answers, "Well, let's just keep walking. I'm not going near the lounge today. It gives me the creeps."

We keep walking toward our classrooms. Reba's classroom is in the same wing as mine and the teacher's lounge. It's before mine so I tell her a half-hearted, "Have a good day and see you for lunch."

Wanda Terrill isn't in her room, and neither is Maybelle Clyde. Oh well, it's only 7:30. Reba and I had arrived early and together after deciding neither one of us wanted to enter the building alone.

I empty my tote bag, put the writing papers on the students' desk and straighten out the desks. I think I am ready for another day but this is unlike any day ever at the school. Our principal is dead. We don't know what happened.

Why is that tape keeping us out of the lounge? Why is the cherry pie out when I'm sure I put it away?

It will be hard to have a normal day with the students. The hum from the intercom breaks my thought pattern. After the hum comes a loud but shaky voice. "Teachers, this is Bill Thomas. I'll be your acting principal until further notice. We will have a short staff meeting at 8:05 a.m. in the conference room. Please be there on time. Thank you."

A few minutes later, Reba appears at my door and says, "What do you think this is all about, Dana? And did you see Wanda Terrill isn't in her room? Have you seen her or Maybelle?"

I answer, "I haven't seen either one of them yet. You know Maybelle may come waltzing in a little late with her usual flair. She thinks she can do what she wants since her husband's on the school board."

Reba continues, "Dana, who's going to clean our rooms? Mr. Bates has been suspended, and we've never heard from him. I'm worried."

I respond, "Well I hope we get some answers at this meeting. Hey let's head down to the conference room."

"Hi Sara." Passing down the hall we see one of our favorite substitutes unlocking Wanda Terrill's classroom door. "Oh, Wanda isn't here?" Reba and I both ask the question in unison. We can tell we have worked a long time together.

Sara answers, "No, Mr. Thomas called this morning at 6:30 and said Wanda had just called in sick, so here I am. He said he had seven teachers call in sick today here at Lincoln. After what happened last night, it doesn't surprise me. I'm a little freaked out myself."

Reba responds, "We all are for sure. Well, see you later. Mr. Thomas has called a staff meeting and we're headed down there."

Sara questions, "Gosh I wonder whether I'm expected to be there? I'll get settled and wander down just in case."

Maybelle's room remains locked and deserted. Did she call in sick too? I wonder.

Arriving at the door of the conference room, we pause. No one is here yet but it's only eight o'clock, and we still have five minutes. We take our usual places. Mine is always on the right side, the first chair. Reba's is on the right side, the second chair. We do have seniority in the building, and this reminds us of our role in the school structure. Our unwritten faculty curriculum dictates where we all sit.

This room usually has a homey feeling. A committee of several of us in charge of beautifying the building decorated it with large silk plants, some soft cushion chairs and a rocker. For today's meeting we know to sit around the large conference room table. The room and the table seem so sterile. The room smells of the sweet pumpkin diffuser we have in the room.

We've figured out that Mr. Caton's death was ruled suspicious. What happened? Did someone hurt Mr. Caton? My mind is racing with questions. What about that car that I saw cruising through the parking lot when I left?

Why is Wanda absent? Even though there were several of us who didn't like Mr. Caton, he was still the principal and it was hard to think that he is dead. I feel a bit guilty about his death. While I didn't like him, I sure didn't want to see him dead.

In a couple of minutes, Maddie arrives. She is one of our lunch bunch and has been here at Lincoln for 6 years. She teaches 4th grade. We call her the sandwich filling. I teach 5th grade, Reba teaches 3rd, and Maddie teaches 4th.

Maddie blurts out, "Can you believe this nightmare? Dana, can we have lunch in your room since the lounge is closed. I don't understand what's going on. Mr. Caton was in good health. He exercised all the time."

I explain to Maddie, "We know the death is suspicious. I can't figure out what happened. He was fine when I left though he sure was mad at me. I filed that report on Wanda hitting the student."

Reba chimes in, "Well let's have lunch in your room, Dana. We should keep our eyes and ears opened today to figure out what's going on. Maybe we'll know more after this meeting."

Here come the primary wing teachers from the K-2 end. They take their designated seats on the other side of the table. The intermediate wing sits on one side and primary sit on the other. A few minutes later, Mr. Thomas walks in very quickly and takes his place at the head of the table and remains standing. While he is trying to act in control, he looks very unsure of himself. Typical administrator can be late, but teachers better not be. Mr. Thomas is probably in his 50s, short; the little bit of hair he has is gray. The frown on his face this morning makes him look even older.

Maybelle never arrives. There is dead silence as Mr. Thomas begins. He clears his throat and coughs a few times. He has a piece of paper and he reads what appears to be a prepared script. "Good morning, staff. First of all let me say how sad I am about all that has happened and our thoughts and prayers go to the Caton family." Oops, the thought comes to my mind; we aren't supposed to talk about prayer in the school.

Mr. Thomas continues, "I appreciate those of you who have come in. We have had to get a number of substitutes because of the number of absences here today. Those are understandable. If students ask questions about Mr. Caton, please tell them that Mr. Caton died last night, and if they would like to talk to our school social worker, Jenny Craig, they can do so."

Jenny Craig has always been a good sport about her name. Jenny has been a social worker here at Lincoln since I arrived and could really use the services of the diet. Such a pretty face and short curly black hair but an extra 80 pounds on that 5' 4" body is just too much.

What an irony that Jenny is going to talk to the students about Caton's death. I know she hated him because he frequently poked fun about her weight. Caton loved to bully the staff, and so many of the staff had been his victims, me included just yesterday.

He was known for calling teachers and other staff into his office and pointing his finger in their faces and telling them everything they did wrong. He would raise his voice in staff meetings so we knew he was in charge.

Mr. Thomas continues, "We'll try to have as normal of a day as possible. After the students leave, I must ask for your cooperation. The police will be here to continue their investigation into Mr. Caton's uh…death. You may be interviewed by them. I must remind you that you are to answer only the questions that they ask. You are not to give any additional information to the police. Our school attorney will be present during the interrogations."

At the word "interrogations" Reba's hand flies up. Teachers are so used to expecting students to raise their hands that they do the same thing. Mr. Thomas nods for her to ask her question.

Reba speaks cautiously. She is very upset, as I am, since the reality that this situation just keeps getting worse is sinking in. "Mr. Thomas, why are the police interrogating us? Mr. Nollwood said that Mr. Caton probably died of a heart attack."

Mr. Thomas's face begins to turn red, and he appears to be thinking about the right words to use. After all, he has been asked something that obviously isn't on his prepared script. "I must inform all of you that even though there is no definitive proof, there is suspicion that his death was not a heart attack. It could be a homicide."

All of us gasp. A homicide at our school. This is a bad dream.

"I must ask all of you to keep this information quiet. You are not to share it with your students or anyone outside this building. I hope all of you understand my message. If I find out that anyone disclosed information to anyone outside this building, there will be serious repercussions. Thank you all for being here today. I trust you all of you will work hard to have as normal of a day as you can." Mr. Thomas walks away from the head of the table and exits the door.

The faculty appears to be shocked and stunned, silence overwhelms us. We all just sit there. The sounds of the bus engines remind us that we have students to teach today. We get up like zombies and walk back to our classrooms. How is it possible to have a normal day?

CHAPTER 4

My stupid classroom door shakes again. It happens when someone knocks. The shaking creates a scare in me every time. Today, even more so, since I'm on edge anyway.

It's only 10:30 and I feel like it should be 5:00. All the students look to the door and then to me to see what I am going to do. Even though there is a small window on the door, it's hard to see who is there so I'm going to have to leave my students' briefly to answer the knock. I announce to my students, "Ladies and gentleman, I would appreciate it if you would continue to work on your math project while I answer the door."

When I open the door, I see the acting principal, Mr. Thomas. He has a scowl on his face. Oh no, now what has happened? What else can go wrong today? I am soon to find out. I just realize how tall he is. It seems like he is towering over me.

Mr. Thomas says in a very agitated tone, "Miss Lawrence, there is a caseworker here from the Department of Children and Family Services. She says she needs to speak with you about a call you made to the Department yesterday. Something about suspected abuse of a student by Mrs. Terrill.

"Oh, what should I do about someone watching my students?" I ask.

"I didn't know what she was talking about." He pauses, "I'm sorry to say. You had better explain this whole thing to me right after school. I don't want to take any unnecessary time out of our instructional day. I'm going to cover your class while you go meet with the

19

caseworker and answer her questions. After school I want to see you in my office."

"Thank you, Mr. Thomas, I'm sorry I haven't had the time to tell you what happened yesterday. I will come down right after school and explain the situation. I need to go back inside and get my notes before I go down to the office. I'll introduce you to my students."

Mr. Thomas comes into my classroom.

"Ladies and Gentleman, thank you for doing your work. I really like the way you are working hard on that math project. This is Mr. Thomas, our acting principal, and he will be filling in for me while I go to a short meeting. I know that you will show him all you are doing." I take my notebook out of my desk and leave the room.

As I walk out of my room and stand in the hall, I am feeling overwhelmed at the thought of being interviewed by the Department of Children and Family Services. I wish it was time to go home. What a day. I pause and take a deep breath.

I then realize I have to get down to the office, so I walk down the hall. As I go by Maybelle's room, I see a substitute teaching since Maybelle must have called in sick. I wish I would have done the same thing but I don't do that. In the last 15 years I have only taken four sick days, one when I scratched my eye with my contact lens, and the other days when my Mom was in the hospital.

Maybelle Clyde is always calling in sick. She has had to use the sick leave bank a couple of times. We all donate an extra sick day or two each year so that someone who has a catastrophic illness can use days from the bank. Maybelle sure hasn't had a catastrophic illness, but she still gets away with using the bank.

When I arrive at the office, I see a matronly lady sitting in the waiting area. She looks to be about 50 years old, although I am no judge of age. Her shoes are what I call old lady school teacher shoes. She has a black skirt on with a pale blue turtleneck. Her wire-rimmed glasses make her look her age and her short hair is graying. Her file folder is in her hand.

Mrs. Depper, the school secretary, looks up and says, "Dana, this is Mrs. Whitten from the Department of Children and Family Services. Mr. Thomas says you can use Mr. Caton's office to talk to her."

I look shocked when she says this, so she adds, "Oh, I'm sorry I mentioned Mr. Caton, I can't believe he's actually dead. I'll be so glad when this day is over."

I introduce myself to Mrs. Whitten and lead her into what was Mr. Caton's office. I get spooked out looking at Mr. Caton's desk and thinking that the last time I was in here was yesterday afternoon when Mr. Caton reemed me because I called the Department of Children and Family Services without checking with him. Mr. Caton wanted to keep all school incidents quiet, and handle them internally, but I am a mandated reporter and am required to report child abuse.

Now here I am with the lady from the Department. We sit in two chairs that face Mr. Caton's desk, but I pull mine away from his desk and see that Mrs. Whitten does the same.

Mrs. Whitten begins by opening her file folder, and taking a pen out and saying, "Ms. Lawrence, I am here to investigate your call about what you saw with Mrs. Terrill. Thank you for taking your responsibility of being a mandated reporter seriously by calling our agency. Please be advised that I have already interviewed Jason and his family, although I can't tell you the results of that interview. Will you tell me exactly what you saw yesterday?"

Thoughts are churning in my mind about what Jason may have said about Mrs. Terrill but I have to focus on telling Mrs. Whitten what I saw.

I open my notebook as I say, "Mrs. Whitten, I wrote down what I saw and what I reported to the hotline. I gave Mr. Caton a copy of my notes before he, uh, died. I had just taken my students to music at 10:30 a.m. and was returning to my room. I was walking down the hall and went by Mrs. Terrill's room. She was raising her voice to Jason and she was yelling at him. The door was open to her room, so I stopped outside the door to see what was going on. I thought maybe I could help. A lot of teachers ask me for help with behavior management. Mr. B. was cleaning a spot off the carpet in the hall, and he also heard the noise. He came down the hall and stood outside the door. We looked in the door."

"Pardon me, Dana, who is Mr. B. and what is his role?"

I answer, "He's our school custodian."

I say, "Mrs. Terrill didn't see us and she just kept yelling at Jason. Jason then called her a name and she slapped him in the face. Both of us saw it."

Mrs. Whitten has a scowl on her face. "What name did Jason call her?"

I pause because I'm not comfortable saying the word in front of somebody I don't know and in a school setting: "He called her a whore."

"What were the other students doing during this whole, uh, altercation?" Mrs. Whitten asked.

I am trying to remember beyond what I had written down. "They were watching the whole thing and not saying a word. I remember that Billy was snickering and Amanda was sobbing."

"What happened after that? Where was Mrs. Terrill in the room that she never saw you?"

"Mrs. Terrill was in the back of the room. She never saw us. She told Jason to go back to his seat and told the rest of the students to continue working. She wanted them to be quiet for the next 15 minutes. No one said another word. Mr. Bates and I left the room. I told Mr. Bates that I would go down and tell Mr. Caton what had happened. I also told Mr. Bates that since we are mandated reporters, we would have to call the Department of Children and Family Services."

"Did Mr. Bates understand that?" Mrs. Whitten asked.

"Yes," I said, "We would talk more after I came back from Mr. Caton's office. Then I came down here and asked to see Mr. Caton. Mrs. Depper told me he was out at a meeting, and wouldn't be back until after school."

"Where was he at a meeting?" Mrs. Whitten asked.

"She didn't say. I was upset and I told her that I needed to reach him right away. She tried to call him on his cell phone but he didn't answer. I went back down the hall, found Mr. Bates, and we went to my room since my kids were still at music. I called the hotline and reported what I told you. Mr. Bates then did the same thing."

Mrs. Whitten thanks me for the information I have provided. She asks, "Is Mr. Bates here, I will need to talk with him next after we finish?"

"Oh, I thought you knew. Didn't Mr. Thomas tell you? Mr. Bates got a call from a school board member telling him that he was suspended from his job yesterday after school. I am concerned, because I haven't been able to reach him. He isn't answering his phone."

"Do you know anywhere he could be so I can interview him?"

"I know his daughter lives here in town, but I don't know how to reach her. She is married, and I think her last name is Gretchen. She works at National Advance Bank."

"I appreciate your help. Do you have any idea why Jason would call Mrs. Terrill a whore?" Does Mrs. Terrill know Jason's family? Has she ever talked to you about Jason's father?"

"No, I'm not a friend of Mrs. Terrill. She doesn't hang around Reba, and me and her lunch period is different than mine, so I don't talk to her very often. She's good friends with Maybelle Clyde, one of the school board member's wife, who also teaches here."

"Dana, thank you for answering my questions. I am continuing this investigation and need to let you know that if you think of any further information that would be helpful to me, I need you to call me right away. Here is my card with my phone number." Mrs. Whitten closes her file folder, looks at me as if she understands how tough this has been for me, and moves toward the door.

She turns and looks at me, "Dana, I know this is very difficult for you but remember that you were doing your job. I wish you the best." She leaves the room, thanks the secretary for her time, and walks out into the hall.

I gather my notebook, pause a minute, thinking that I should feel relieved that the interview is over.

Instead I feel even worse. What is happening to me? Just yesterday morning, I was happy in my fifth grade classroom; now twenty four hours later I have seen a child get hit, had to report it, get called in to the principal's office, find out the principal was found dead, and now have made the acting principal mad. I have gotten myself in a real mess. I have to get back to my classroom, so I walk back by Mrs. Depper's desk.

The office is empty except for Mrs. Depper, who is curious, "Is everything okay, Dana, what's going on, you don't look so good? Can you believe everything that has happened here since yesterday?"

"I'll be fine. That was just a hard meeting to have. I can't believe it all. I have to get back to class. I'll talk to you later." I have always been careful about what I say to Mrs. Depper. For some reason, I have never trusted her. She loves to talk about one teacher to another, and I never know what she would say to the acting principal.

After being in the building for 15 years, I have learned what I can say to whom.

I head down the hall with my head spinning. Why did Mrs. Whitten ask me whether Mrs. Terrill knew Jason's family? What did she mean when she asked whether Wanda Terrill ever talked about Jason's father?

CHAPTER 5

"I'm not sure you should meet with Mr. Thomas without a union representative," Reba cautioned me as we meet for lunch.

Maddie, part of our lunch bunch, has joined us as has Sara, the substitute who is filling in for Wanda. Sara is a regular sub in our building. She is probably in our building three days a week. Her husband is big in the business community, and she sure doesn't have to work, but she loves to teach part time. She makes her classrooms fun when she is at our school. Her three boys are in college now; she has always been active in volunteer work.

Maddie adds, "Remember when that jerky principal three years ago was coming on to me, I notified the union right away and they were very helpful to me. They met with the superintendent and principal and he quit making passes at me."

I reply, "I don't know what to do. I left a text message for Jessica, the union president yesterday. I'm going to try to reach her again right now." I pick up my cellphone and punch in her number.

She answers this time on the second ring. "Hi, Dana, sorry I haven't called you back. With everything that's going on, I've been swamped. What's up today?"

I explain that Mr. Thomas is upset about the call I made to DCFS yesterday and told me to meet with him this afternoon, "Should I meet with him without a union representative?"

There is a brief pause on the other end. Jessica replies slowly, "Dana, I have to tell you that Wanda Terrill has also contacted me. She says you and Mr. Bates made the whole thing up. Maybelle, her dear friend, has also told me you made it up. Are you really that jealous of Wanda?"

My face is red; my blood pressure must be through the roof. I respond with a raised voice, "Well, isn't that interesting that Wanda and Maybelle had time to call you? They both are out sick today."

I pause, "I most certainly did not make it up. Are you telling me you are taking Maybelle and Wanda's word over mine?"

Reba and Sara's mouths drop open.

Jessica responds over the phone, "Now Dana, that is not what I am saying at all, but I want to make you aware that we're in a tough spot right now. Our responsibility is to thoroughly investigate what really happened and then decide what to do to be fair to all of you."

By now I am steaming, and my voice is louder, "Well, what about fair to the student who was hit? You're telling me that you won't represent me until you've seen whose story you're going to believe. What am I supposed to do this afternoon?"

"Dana, let me make a couple of calls and see what I can find out. When is your lunch time over?"

"In about twenty minutes," I say in an irritated tone.

"I promise you, I'll call you back before that."

"I sure hope so. Thanks."

I put the cellphone down and look at Reba, "Can you believe that. The union has already been contacted by Wanda and Maybelle.

Reba looks at me and says, "I don't believe it. No wonder you're mad. They probably took the day off so they could plan their defense. What's Jessica going to do?"

"She said they are investigating and then will decide," I say. "She said she will call me back in twenty minutes. I'm not holding my breath. Wonder whether she was ever going to call me back or just ignore me."

Maddie chimes in, "I knew Jessica was going to be a bad union president. I wish I would have decided to run against her, but I really didn't think she would win against Bart over at Jefferson School. "

Sara is sitting there listening to this whole exchange. "I can't believe Jessica is not doing anything for you."

Reba continues, "Tell us what happened with the DCFS caseworker."

I recount the meeting with Mrs. Whitten and then add, "Mrs. Whitten asked something strange. She asked me whether Wanda was familiar with Jason's father. I have been trying to figure out what she meant."

Reba adds, "Don't you remember that I told you I heard Wanda complaining a lot about her husband when she was in the teacher's lounge? She is always saying he just doesn't appreciate her enough."

Sara speaks up, "I guess he doesn't appreciate her. Why would he?" I heard she's been having an affair for the last two months. My husband has a good friend who works with Wanda's husband, and he told him he was going to leave her if she didn't break the whole thing off."

Reba, Maddie, and I gasp. We hadn't heard anything about an affair. Reba heard she was never happy with what she had.

"Her husband has been stressed out about her behavior for a long time, because she is never satisfied," Sara adds. "He can't work hard enough to keep her happy." You know he bought her that new house two years ago thinking that would make her happy but it didn't."

Reba adds, "Oh my goodness, Sara, you certainly have given us an earful. I always wondered why her husband stayed with her. She might be good looking and know what to wear to accent what she's got, but she's never content. Now that their daughter is married and left home, Wanda has too much time on her hands. She and Maybelle are a good pair. They think they are god's gift to men, and better than the rest of us."

Maddie chimes in, "Wait a minute. Do you think she could be having an affair with Jason's father? Jason's last name is Estes." She looks at Sara, "Can you find out the name of the person Wanda's having the affair with? We need to find out whether it's Jason's father? "

Sara says, "Sure, I'll check to see if my hubbie has ever heard a name mentioned. I'll call you tonight after I talk to him."

CHAPTER 6

The marching music starts playing while we eat our lunch. It's my cell phone again. I thought the sound would be a great ring for the phone but now what a fool I was. What I don't need right now is this noise. I feel like I'm marching to the guillotine.

I think the call is from Jessica. I am impressed she is calling back so quick, "Yes, Dana here."

Ashton, my boyfriend, is talking fast. I know he's worried and upset, "Dana, are you okay? My god, I can't believe what has happened. First the rape, now your school."

"Ashton, slow down, I'm doing okay, how are you?" I reply.

"I was up most of the night on the rape case, then crashed," Ashton says. "I came in to the station a couple of hours ago and heard about the school. I knew I couldn't get you until your lunch hour."

I answer staying as calm as I can. "Oh, Ashton, it's crazy here. A lot of teachers called in sick because the principal is dead. I saw one of the teachers hit a student yesterday, and when I reported it to Caton, he chewed me out and told me I really didn't see it. DCFS was here this morning to interview me."

"Why did DCFS interview you?" Ashton asks.

"Standard procedure when anyone files a complaint, they have to get the details," I say and take a breath. "The lounge is tied off with police tape. And on top of that, we're going to be interviewed by the police this afternoon." I realize I am talking non-stop.

"I'm so sorry I haven't been there for you," Ashton says.

I keep going, "Now the acting principal, Mr. Thomas, wants to meet with me. He's mad about the report to DCFS so I'm trying to get the union to be present when I meet with Thomas."

"Good idea."

"What a mess. I keep thinking I'll wake up, and it's all a bad dream," I pause a few seconds. "Oh, Ashton, I'm rambling on about what happened to me and haven't even asked what's going on with your rape investigation. I watched the story on the news last night."

Reba's in the background telling me to ask Ashton what he knows.

Ashton hears her and replies, "Dana, I can't say much. Since I'm on the rape case and since I'm dating you, I'm not going to be on the Lincoln/Caton case."

"Oh darn. I have faith you could solve the murder," I mumble.

Ashton comments, "Dana, I'm worried like crazy about you. Why are you having the union present for your meeting with Thomas and not having the union's attorney with you when you're interrogated by the police?"

"Hold it, Ashton, that's taken care of," I say, "The school board attorney is going to be present when we are questioned. Why are you asking me that?"

"Dana, the school board can get rid of you if they don't like what you say. They may not be able to do it right away but they can hold anything you say against you and use it later. You just told me you had motive—you were upset with Caton. "

"Sure, I was upset with him, but I wouldn't murder him," I say.

"Dana, please get the union rep. or their attorney to go with you when you're questioned." The alarm in Ashton's voice has me worried.

"Oh, nobody's going to think I would do anything to Caton. I don't have anything to hide." But doubt is now clouding my mind.

"Dana, I know you have nothing to hide but please I've got to tell you to be very careful. Hey, hon, I gotta go. I'm coming over tonight, and I'll bring dinner. We have to talk more. Call the union."

My stomach churns as I say, "Thanks, Ashton, I'll talk to the union again. See you tonight."

Sara gives me a concerned look, "Dana, what's wrong? You're really pale. What did Ashton say?"

Reba chimes in, "This doesn't sound good."

I get up and throw the rest of my sandwich away. Somehow, looking at and smelling the turkey on whole wheat makes me want to throw up.

"Ashton said I could be a suspect, because I had a motive after my altercation with Caton." My voice is lower, because I'm afraid somebody will hear me.

Reba keeps hers low and says, "Oh, no, I never thought about that. You know most of us could be accused of having a motive, because we all hated Caton's guts, They couldn't think a teacher would kill somebody."

She pauses, then says, "Wait a minute. Maybe we all better have the union present, and it shouldn't be that useless Jessica. It should be the union's attorney. I'm calling Barry right now." Reba's husband, Barry, is an attorney although he specializes in real estate law.

Reba pulls out her cellphone, punches in the number on her speed dial. She says, "Barry, can you talk a minute? I'll make it quick." She gives him an update.

As I hear her tell what's happened, my upset stomach returns. That turkey taste is killing me. She's listening intently and not saying anything. Soon she blurts out, "Oh my god, I'll get to work. Thanks."

After hearing the closing conversation, I'm beginning to shake and ask, "What did Barry say?"

Reba is already punching in numbers on her phone and puts her finger up to tell me to be quiet. "I'm calling Jessica. Barry says this is serious, and we have to have a union attorney present."

"Jessica, this is Reba Krell at Lincoln. You know we are being interrogated over here about Caton's death. The school board attorney is going to be present, and I want the union attorney present. I won't take no for an answer." There is a pause, and Reba listens to Jessica's response.

"Well, I'm glad other people have called you with the same request," Reba continues. "We'll expect to see the union attorney this afternoon. Thanks, Jessica."

Reba looks at Sara and me, "Barry told me that under no circumstances was I going to talk to the police without an attorney present, and, if the union for which we pay those big dues, would not represent us we would hire an attorney and send the union the bill."

I answer, "Oh my god, this is just too much to assimilate. Everything has happened so fast my head is spinning."

Marching music makes me jump. Maybe I ought to put a calmer ring on my phone, especially now with all that's going on. I answer a bit sharply, "Dana here."

On the other end of the phone, "Dana, it's Jessica, the union attorney and I will be there right after school dismissal for the police interrogation. The attorney will also be meeting with Mr. Thomas to recommend that his meeting with you be postponed until the police interviews are over, and when it is mutually agreeable for you, the union attorney, and Mr. Thomas to meet."

"Thanks, Jessica, glad that decision has been made," I answer.

Jessica says, "Our attorney, Pat Glascoe, will want to set up a meeting with you about the incident you said you saw yesterday. "

I interrupt Jessica because I have to correct her, "Jessica, I know what I saw, and you should know I would never make up something like that."

Jessica interrupts me, "Dana, haven't you heard that this thing with Wanda is serious. She was just arrested about an hour ago for hitting Jason Estes."

I am stunned. "How and why was she arrested? "

Jessica answers, "Jason's mother pressed charges against Wanda, and it seems that Bates has been located and interviewed. He has signed a statement about what he saw. Guess you are going to have several interviews with the police. Good luck."

Jessica hangs up. I just stare at my phone. What a lunch break this has been.

CHAPTER 7

The afternoon creeps by. Even with the hands-on science activity I planned and our social studies lesson on the early settlers which is one of my favorite topics, I sure wasn't myself even though, "Act normal, Act normal." The internal voice keeps playing over and over in my head. I just can't shake my apprehension about what I am in for after school.

One of my students, Kendra, asks as we are lining up to go home, "Miss Lawrence, why are you so sad today? Did we do something wrong?" Kendra is my little protective hen, always wanting to know if everything is okay.

"Thanks for asking, Kendra, I've got some things on my mind but I'm okay. Can't wait to hear tomorrow about your visit to your grandma's tonight. Have a good time. "

I try to deflect Kendra's focus away from me to what she has to look forward to tonight.

I plaster a smile on my face as I tell all my students to have a great evening. As we go down the hall toward the school entrance, we have to pass by the teacher's lounge. Thank goodness the door is shut so the students can't see the police tape.

I see the kids off on the bus and watch two of the kids get in cars to go home. A voice in my head says, "Thank goodness, I made it through the day."

Sara says, Thank god we made it through this day." We just stand there on the school steps trying to process this day from hell.

Reba arrives with her students. "Thanks, guys, for walking so quietly in the hall." She is handing out the little white slips to her students who have walked down the hall appropriately. Tomorrow the white slips will go in the jar, and there will be a drawing in the afternoon for a special treat. Sara and I completely forgot to praise our kids, even though they had been very quiet going down the hall.

    The kids had really been good today. Even though Caton didn't connect well with the students, they still had to be bothered by his death. Caton never seemed to take a personal interest in the students and he stayed in his office as much as possible. He only talked to the students when he had to. None of my students had asked to see the social worker.

    Reba looks at Sara, "Hey, was Jason Estes at school today?"

    Sara replies quickly, "He wasn't here. Thank goodness. Have I got lots to tell you, but we better wait til we get some place private. You won't believe it. "

    Reba, Sara, and I wander back to Reba's room this time. We would usually stop at the teacher's lounge for a break while congratulating ourselves for making it through another day.

    Can't do that today. We head to Reba's room.

    Reba's got water bottles and crystal light packets, so we treat ourselves. Reba has served each of us as we are seated at the round table in her room. She blurts out, "Sara, tell us what happened today?"

    Sara explains, "I was going to tell you some of it at lunch, but there was too much going on. Anyway, it was a rough day. The kids kept wanting to talk about what they saw yesterday, and I kept having to tell them that we have to get our assignments done before Mrs. Terrill gets back. One of the kids actually said, "Mrs. Terrill can't come back, she hit Jason, and my mother said teachers can't hit students."

Sara's eyes have dark circles under them. "I gotta tell you I didn't know what to say, so I just kept going on with my math lesson. And speaking of math, Wanda left no lesson plans for math or anything. I had to punt all day. What a mess."

I blurt out, "Oh, Sara, how awful. You should let Thomas know, especially if you're going to be in that class for any long period of time."

Sara says, "I am going to let Thomas know, since so many people think Wanda is wonderful. Can you imagine how that image is going out the window when people find out she's been arrested. I don't mind subbing, and I don't mind doing the lesson plans, but I sure don't want Thomas to think that Wanda has done any of the lesson plans." The disgust in her voice is obvious.

"Well, doesn't that figure," I grumble. "Wanda doesn't do her lesson plans. She hits a student. I am appalled by her behavior. Why would she do such an awful thing?"

"The students also said Jason had been making fun of Mrs. Terrill all day yesterday," Sara adds.

"What are you talking about?" Reba asks. "Was he calling her names?"

"According to the class leader, Bethanne, Jason kept saying, "My mother wants you to leave my dad alone."

Reba and I gasp in surprise. Reba asks, "What did he mean? What is going on with Wanda and Jason's father? Is Wanda playing around with him?"

I say, "Well, that makes sense about why Jason's mother would press charges against Wanda. Sounds like Wanda has put herself in a big mess. Course, guess we're in a mess too."

Sara says, "Can you believe this whole thing? I will keep my ears open tomorrow and see what is said."

"Do you think we ought to head down to the office, or wait until we're called?" I ask.

Reba responds, "Good question. I don't know what we ought to do."

The intercom starts buzzing. Even though all three of us hear that sound multiple times every day, we jump. Our nerves are on edge.

The loud voice of Mr. Thomas bellows from the box. "Teachers, if there are any students still in the building, please call down to the office right away and let me know who the student is and at what time the student will be leaving. Please listen for additional announcements shortly."

"Well I guess that answers our question, we will just have to sit here and wait," Sara says. "Hey, where's Maddie?"

I answer, "Maddie had a student who was staying after school awhile so she could help him with his math. She's been working with him for about a week now after school. Wonder if the student has left yet?"

Sara answers, "I wonder how long we'll have to stay today. I have to pick something up at four thirty, so hope we don't have a long wait. Frankly, I am exhausted from this day. I know you guys have to be also."

I reply, "Boy, that's an understatement. I feel like I can't move much more. I'm so tired. Sara, I wonder whether you will even have to meet with the police at all."

The hum from the wall comes back. Mr. Thomas announces, "Teachers and all staff: "I will be calling as many of you to the office as possible, but one at a time. When I call your name, please report to the office immediately. I will let all of you know when you are free to leave for the day. I ask that Dana Lawrence report to the school office right away."

Reba looks at me. I'm scared. She says quietly, "Good luck, Dana, let's wait for each other here until we're told we can leave."

"Thanks, Reba. Good idea, I feel like I'm going to the firing squad. See you guys later."

I grab my notebook and head out the door and down the hallway, the fear and apprehension of what awaits me makes me feel like I am carrying all my worries in a backpack strapped to my shoulders.

CHAPTER 8

Mrs. Depper, our school secretary, looks up at me as I enter the office door. She always has a reed diffuser on her desk. This one is pumpkin, one of my favorite smells, but it doesn't seem to comfort me today.

To make people feel welcome, she always has a jar full of candy kisses. Those even cause my stomach to churn, and I love chocolate. "Dana, you can go on in the principal's office. Everybody is waiting there. I've already been through the whole ordeal."

I answer, "Can't believe I'm called into the principal's office twice in two days. "I'm trying to make a joke to relieve my stress. "Who is everybody?"

"There are several people here. Good luck, Dana."

As I walk in to the office, I see several people. The room seems so sterile. It's an overcast fall day so even with the windows. The room is dreary looking. Mr. Thomas is sitting at the Principal's desk, which is so large that it overpowers the room.

Assistant Chief of Police, Bob Unger, is there. I recognize him. There are advantages of dating a police officer. I pretty much know the entire police force. Unger has a chair pulled up to the principal's desk and has his small notebook open.

Sitting on the other side of Thomas is the school board attorney, Don Moss. I have heard him address the school board and have seen him interviewed on TV. In another chair is Jessica, the union representative and next to her is another woman I don't recognize.

Thomas says in a stern voice, "Come in, Dana, and have a seat," Thomas points to the vacant chair in the center of the room. Nothing like feeling you are in the center of the firing line.

Thomas introduces me to everyone and I learn the unrecognized woman is Pat Glascoe, the union attorney. Glascoe looks to be about 50 years old, blank expression on her face, mousy short brown hair, and dressed in Chico's travelers clothes. I always wonder why people wear travelers clothes when they're really not traveling except across town. She is short, perfect weight for her height.

The school board attorney and Pat Glascoe stand up to shake my hand.

Assistant Chief Unger explains: "Miss Lawrence, I'm going to need to ask you some questions. We'll all go across the hall to the conference room."

I am taken aback because I expected to stay in the principal's office to be interviewed.

I respond quietly, "Okay."

Back to that conference room again where we were this morning. I take a seat in the same chair I had this morning. The voices in my head keep saying, "Remain calm, just answer the questions they ask and no more."

It sure would have been helpful if the union attorney would have met with me ahead of time, but so be it. I open my notebook and it gives me a slight feeling of security. I feel like I'm organized and prepared for anything.

Assistant Chief Unger opens his questioning, "Ms. Lawrence, we believe you were one of the last people to see Mr. Caton alive. Can you tell us about the meeting you had with him yesterday afternoon?"

I explain as clear and precisely as I can what the meeting was about yesterday afternoon and what had precipitated the meeting.

Unger continues, "Ms. Lawrence, was Mr. Caton upset with you?"

I answer calmly, "Yes."

"Would you say you were upset with him?"

I admit, "Yes, I was upset because he didn't appear to believe me."

"Where did you go after you left his office?"

I outline my evening saying that I had gone back to my classroom, got some materials to take home, and went home for the evening.

"What time did you leave the building?"

"I left about 4:30 p.m."

"Were you with anyone last night?"

"No, I spent the evening at home."

"Can anyone verify that you were at home all evening?"

"I talked to my mother on the phone and also talked to Reba, my good friend, and then later I received the call about Mr. Caton's death."

Unger continues, "But no one was with you at your home last night that can verify you were there?"

I answer: "No." I am feeling now that I am in a heap of trouble. I don't have an alibi for where I was last night.

The Unger interrogation doesn't end, "Did you notice anything unusual last night when you left?"

"I remember that another car was pulling out of the parking lot when I left. I didn't recognize the car though since it was beginning to get dark."

Unger replies, "Do you remember anything about the car?"

"It looked to be a fairly new car, medium size, and it was white. I didn't see the license plate but it looked like a Toyota Camry but I'm not sure."

"Ms. Lawrence, did you see Mr. Bates when you left last night?"

"I didn't see him in the building when I left." I am figuring they already know he was suspended from work and I'm not going to say anymore than I have to about Mr. Bates.

"Ms. Lawrence, one more question. Do you know anything about the cherry pie that was in the lounge?" Did you make it?"

"No, I'm not a big baker but it was sitting out in the teacher's lounge when I got ready to leave so I put it in the refrigerator in the lounge. This morning the pie was out again. I thought that was strange."

"How much of the pie was there when you put it away?

"There was about half of it left when I put it away but come to think of it, this morning, there were only about two pieces left of the cherry pie."

"Miss Lawrence, thank you for cooperating. You are free to go. Please be advised you may be called in for further questioning."

I ask, "Thanks, will you let us know what will be happening next?" My curiosity is getting the best of me.

Unger doesn't seem to like my question because he gets a frown on his face, "Miss Lawrence, while this case is under investigation we will be asking more questions than giving answers. We hope we can solve the case soon to bring justice to Mr. Caton and his family. Good evening"

Mr. Thomas has walked out of the room ahead of me and I follow along. He goes back into the office.

While I am headed back to Reba's room, I hear the intercom, "Sara Preston, please report to the conference room at once."

CHAPTER 9

On my nightly phone call to Mother as I drive home, I say "Mother, it's a mess right now. I was interviewed by the police today as were several of the staff members. The police are saying that they believe Caton's death was a homicide. Since I may have been the last one to see him alive, I am being questioned."

Mother raises her voice, "Homicide? Oh my goodness, Dana, that school is not safe at all. Is Ashton coming over tonight? I will feel better if you aren't alone."

She has already heard some of the information on the news and the grapevine here in Hallicott City. News travels fast in our town especially among mother's friends who are retired, and who pride themselves in knowing everything.

"Yes, Ashton is coming over tonight and bringing pizza but he said he isn't allowed to say much, because the case is pending. He's not assigned to this since he's working on that rape case. I will call you if I hear anything else. Have a great time at your card club tonight."

I still can't believe that I am a suspect in a homicide. I am a teacher, for god's sake. How could a teacher murder anyone? Then I remember that case a couple of years ago where the teacher strangled his wife. So much for the innocence of teachers.

The marching music on my phone goes off again. I answer, "Hi, Ashton, what time are you planning to come over? 6 o'clock will work just great. Right now I feel like it's 10 o'clock. The day was so bad and I hate that it gets dark so early." I pause, "Ashton, I can't wait to see you."

44

It will be so good to see Ashton tonight. I need his comfort. Even though he can't give me any information, he can listen to what I have to say and maybe give me some of his insight. Ashton has been on the police force for 15 years here and has worked himself up from patrolman to lieutenant. We have been dating for two years, but after the jerk I dated before Ashton, I have been hesitant to get too serious about him.

As I get out of my car in the condo garage and have to walk a short distance inside to get into my building, I shiver and the wind is howling. It seems to have picked up since I left school. It is eery and I wonder what is going to happen to me.

As I walk into my dark condo, I can't shake this fear. I turn the lights on in my living area, and look around. I'm worried that maybe someone else is in my apartment. It's good to be home, but I'm still being cautious.

I kick off my shoes and turn on the TV in my living area. I want to hear voices. I walk to the kitchen, turn on the light and go to the frig to get my standard Diet Coke. From the living room, I hear, "Breaking News. "School personnel were questioned today in the death of James Caton. Stay tuned for the Channel six news."

Oh no, now am I going to be on the news? I sit down to listen and just as I do, the doorbell rings. I jump and then realize that it's probably Ashton.

From the other side of the closed door, I hear, "Hey Dana, it's Ashton."

I go to the door quickly, open it, greet him with a quick kiss, and say, "The news is coming on about us being questioned by the police." Ashton has brought pizza for us for dinner. He puts the pizza down on the dining room table in my living area and we both sit down on the couch to listen to what the news commentator says.

A picture of our school flashes on the screen, along with a picture of Caton. The news announcer relays to everybody viewing, "It is believed that James Caton, Principal at Lincoln School, was a murder victim. Today several staff members were questioned about his death. We are waiting for confirmation about who those individuals are."

The announcer pauses briefly, "In another development at the school, Wanda Terrill was arrested on a charge of striking a student on school grounds yesterday. She was released tonight on bond. More after this local message. "A picture of Wanda leaving the jail is flashed on the screen.

I look at Ashton as I say, "Ashton, this is terrible, what a bad name for our school."

Ashton hugs me. I'm so glad he is here. As he pulls away, he says, "Dana, don't worry, everything 's going to be okay."

The news commentator continues, "Neither Bill Thomas, acting principal, or Alfonse Nollwood, school board president, were available for comment. Anonymous sources close to the activities within the school have revealed to WQQT that Bob Bates, longtime custodian at the school, was suspended by Caton yesterday. In another unrelated story, police report a new lead in the rape two days ago on 17th Street. The victim is not being revealed to protect her right to privacy and because of her age."

Ashton appears on the TV screen being interviewed by a reporter and comments, "We have a new lead in this terrible rape that we hope will put the rapist behind bars." I think of how handsome and authoritative Ashton looks on the screen.

The reporter continues, "Can you tell us anything about this lead?"

Ashton answers, "I'm not at liberty to say. We are pursuing the lead and feel confident we will be able to make an arrest within the next two days."

Ashton and the reporter go off the air and are replaced by the news anchor. "Thanks, Katie, stay tuned right here at WQQT for more news."

I turn to Ashton and say, "Good for you, Ashton, I sure hope you catch the rapist." I feel very proud of my boyfriend.

Ashton can't say much about the case but adds, "We were so lucky. We got a big break on the case, and sorry Dana, but I'm going to have to go back to work after we have our pizza. I am so concerned about you."

I flap my hand as I say, "Don't worry about me, I'll be fine after a good night's sleep."

Ashton smiles and says, "It was important to me to get over here and talk with you and see how you're feeling. Hey, the pizza is calling, I got the works because I thought you needed a little bit of everything after the day you had."

I have to admit that the wonderful smell of the pizza is enticing me. I love the smell of the tomato sauce with sausage. I go into the kitchen and get some plates, forks, knives and napkins, and set the table for us on the table in my living area. Usually I would make a salad but I had so much on my mind, I didn't even think about making one. Ashton seems to understand and doesn't say a word.

Ashton says in a very soft voice, "Tell me about your day."

I tell him how the questioning went, and also relay about how the cherry pie was missing some of the pieces, or one very large piece, from last night until today.

The marching music on my phone starts. I grab the phone, "Mr. Bates, where are you? I've been worried sick. I guess you heard everything that has happened. "

I listen to Mr. Bates tell me that he went out of town when he was suspended from his job. After he heard everything that happened, he was afraid that he would be a suspect and better come back. He says he is going to go down to the police station, and let the police question him.

"Oh, Mr. Bates, don't you think you better have an attorney present when you talk to the police?"

Mr. Bates says, "I have nothing to hide. I hope you're okay. Remember that we did the right thing reporting Wanda. I'll call you tomorrow."

He hangs up. He seems determined to let the police know what happened.

Ashton looks at me and says, "You advised Mr. Bates right, he should have an attorney present. You're all suspects, and both you and Mr. Bates had a motive to murder Caton. Caton suspended Mr. Bates, and he chewed you out. I haven't heard anyone else who has a motive to kill Caton."

"Ashton, lots of people had a motive to do away with Caton. He puts us all down in one way or another. He used to make snide comments about Jenny Craig being fat. Mrs. Depper was ticked off at him because she couldn't get accurate records on the money in the student activity fund. Actually I don't know anybody who really liked him."

Ashton raises his eyebrows when I mention the student activity money. "Dana, do you know if Mrs. Depper was interviewed this afternoon?"

I answer, "If she was interviewed she didn't say. I don't know who else was interviewed besides me, Sara, Maddie, and Reba. Of course Wanda wasn't because she was being arrested, and Maybelle didn't show up for school today,"

"This whole thing with Wanda is unbelievable," Ashton comments.

"Oh, wait til you hear what Sara found out about Wanda," I say. "Sara subbed in Wanda's class today and said the kids were talking about Mrs. Terrill, and that the reason she hit Jason was because he said he wanted her to leave his dad alone."

"Jason's last name is Estes, isn't it?" Ashton asks, although it appears he already knows the answer.

"Sure, it's Jason Estes and his mother then pressed the charges against Wanda," I respond.

Ashton is silent, finishes chewing his last piece of pizza, and says, "Dana, I have to go. Thanks for this information."

I'm puzzled by the change in Ashton's attitude, "Ashton, what's wrong? Did I say something I shouldn't have said?"

"You didn't say anything wrong. You just added a piece to this puzzle I'm trying to solve. Gotta go."

CHAPTER 10

Reba and I arrive at the in-service in the large multi-purpose room at our school, and stop in the restroom before the workshop begins.

Maybelle says as she looks at me, "I'm surprised you would have the nerve to show up for this in-service after all the trouble you've caused in our school. Poor Wanda. Now you're a strong suspect in Caton's murder. Let's see if that boyfriend of yours can get you out of this mess."

I am so shocked I am speechless but the fearless Reba takes her on. "For somebody who hasn't shown up for work for the last few days, and has a friend who was arrested I wouldn't be saying anything, Maybelle. Keep your unfounded opinions to yourself and try teaching awhile." Reba pauses and then continues, "Hmm, maybe you can learn something today at this in-service. Come on, Dana, let's get a seat."

Reba finishes with Maybelle and takes me by the arm to go to the multi-purpose room for another potentially boring in service on teaching writing.

I get up my nerve, look at Maybelle, and say, "Just a minute, Maybelle, it seems to me you ought to look in your own mirror. Being friends with someone who hit a child doesn't speak so well for you. If I recall you hated Cayton as much as anybody so you sure had motive to kill him." I turn to Reba, "Now Reba let's go find a seat for this exciting in-service."

We leave Maybelle behind staring at us with her mouth hanging open; surprised we've had the nerve to talk back to her.

Maybelle is used to everyone bowing to her presence because, after all, she is a school board member's wife and everyone just goes along with her. Reba and I are both sick and tired of her games.

She sure isn't the best teacher in the building. If the truth was told, she may be down at the bottom. She flaunts her beauty with the men and lets everyone know who her husband is. I can't stand her behavior. She loves to wear short skirts, daring necklines, and loads of make-up.

On the way to find our seats for the in-service, we bump into Jenny Craig, the social worker. Jenny says, "Do you guys want a roll or doughnut, they're great? I was in charge of the refreshments and made sure we had some good ones for this meeting."

I haven't had much of an appetite lately after all that has happened. Just the sight of the donuts makes me want to throw up. I don't want to be rude so I just say, "No thanks, Jenny, but they do look yummy."

Jenny continues, "I figured we all needed them, and we might as well stretch our stomachs to get prepared for Thanksgiving."

It doesn't seem possible that Thanksgiving is tomorrow. With all the trouble that has happened here at school, my mind has not been on the holiday. I will spend tomorrow at my Mother's, and my brother and family will join us. I hope Ashton will get to come over sometime, depending on his work schedule. I know I will be inundated with lots of questions about everything at school. It is all people seemed to be talking about. After all, how many times is a principal of a school murdered?

Jenny adds, "I always have a big appetite when I'm stressed. My stress level is at an all time high right now. Do you know what that Maybelle said to me this morning?"

"Hard to tell," Reba blurts, "She seems to be on a roll today."

"She told me that everyone knows I hated Cayton because he reminded me all the time that I have a weight problem. The nerve. Can you imagine?"

"What did you say to her?" I ask.

"I told her that was a terrible thing to say, and that I wouldn't dream of killing anybody. She should keep her accusations to herself."

I continue, "I'm sorry, Jenny, she dug her nails in to me too saying I was a suspect also, so join the crowd. Hey, let's go get a seat, I see our acting principal, Bill Thomas, moving to the front like he's ready to introduce the speaker."

We move toward the middle of the room, moving past Maybelle, and find some seats. Maybelle is sitting in the front of the room. She likes to act like she is Queen of Lincoln.

We find our seats and just as we sit down, the acting principal, Bill Thomas, begins his introduction of the speaker.

We learn that our speaker on writing has three years as a classroom teacher and thirteen years as a university professor. She is considered an expert in writing. Well, let's hope so because I'm not in the mood to hear a boring speaker today. I'm hoping she just lectures, because I'm in no mood to participate in small group activities. One thing I sure don't want to do is to be in a group with Maybelle.

Luckily the in-service is supposed to be over by one o'clock, so I only have to sit here four hours. I'm always open to new writing ideas. I'm thinking positively. Maybe I will learn something today that I can use in my classroom.

The speaker spends the next twenty minutes going over the basics of writing. It's time for me to tune out.

My mind is wandering. Who could have killed Cayton? Why haven't the police found anything? Who was driving through the parking lot that night? What about the cherry pie? Wasn't there half the pie left that night but the next day there were only two pieces?

I come back to attention when I hear the speaker tell each of us to jot down a writing prompt we use and then she will ask for volunteers to share their ideas. I look down at my iphone and see that 45 minutes has passed. I have no clue what the speaker has said during most of the time.

At least I know about writing prompts so I write down two of the most popular I use. She then asks us to share and there are about six volunteers. I raise my hand and share my two prompts. These are two my students love. What is the nicest thing anyone ever did for you? Pretend like you are going to the moon, describe the items you will take with you, and why you will take them?

Maybelle turns around and glares at me. Her hand goes up as she shares an idea, a stupid one. Then she turns around and smirks at me.

The speaker gives us a five minute stretch break which turns into twenty minutes. Everyone is complaining about the temperature of the room. It is hot and several people have requested that the temperature be turned down.

When she starts her lecture again, my mind returns to the night of the murder. Whose car was that going through the parking lot? Why did Mr. Bates disappear? There are lots of unanswered questions. How do the puzzle pieces fit together? I can be in big trouble since I saw Cayton last (or maybe not) and had an altercation with him.

The way I see it is that I can just sit and wait it out. That means I may be going to jail, even though I'm innocent. I have read about innocent people spending time in prison for things they didn't do. Am I going to let that happen or am I going to start sniffing around and see what I can find out? It's time for me to be assertive. The next thing I hear is the applause from the audience signaling that another exciting in-service is over.

Reba looks at me, "Wow, Dana, you sure were deep in thought. What were you thinking about?"

I reply, "So much is going through my mind right now."

Reba asks, "Are you going to try some of the writing ideas when we get back from Thanksgiving?"

I come back to reality again. "Hey Reba, how would you like to do some detective work with me?"

CHAPTER 11

I arrive at Mom's house for our annual Thanksgiving Day dinner. I need some sense of order, beauty, and stability. I see it in Mom's already set table.

I comment to my Mother, "Mother, your table setting looks more beautiful every year." The antique baby blue plates and cups and saucers have been in our family for more than seventy years. Mom has told me that someday they will be mine. I worry I may never get to enjoy them if I go to prison for a crime I didn't commit.

We'll be a smaller group this year. My brother, Bud, and his wife Shelley will be here with their son, Alex, my favorite and only 12 year old nephew. Usually my aunt and uncle come but this year they had a chance to go on a cruise. I hope Ashton, my boyfriend, who is a detective in the police department, will arrive for our 2:00 dinner time. He can't guarantee that he will be able to come at all since he is heading the investigation of the rape last week over on 17th Street.

Mother looks at me, and with concern in her voice, says, "Dana, how are you holding up? Do they know anything yet about Caton? Bud is eager to grill you because he's heard lots of things around town. Shelley's told him he shouldn't bother you by asking you questions but he is your big brother, and he's worried too."

In his insurance business, my brother, Bud, always seems to be in the know since he meets so many people in our community. He is active in our local Chamber, which is really a social organization here in town, rather than a business oriented one. Even though our community has over 30,000 residents, it really is a small town with a nosy Chamber membership.

I answer, "Oh, Mother, I wish they would find the killer and we could put this whole thing behind us. I'm going to be doing a little snooping around myself, and Reba said she would help. I decided that I had to do something so that the murderer could be caught and I would be cleared in the whole thing."

Mother gasps, "You are going to do no such thing, Dana. Let the police do their job. I hope they find the killer soon."

"I sure hope so too. If Ashton can solve the rape case, maybe they can put him on this murder and he can figure it all out. I hope Ashton can get here today."

Mother gets back to the dinner at hand, "Hey, can you help me with the dressing now. The salads you brought look great."

The TV on in the kitchen with the Macy's Day Thanksgiving Day parade is a tradition in our family. I always get so excited when Santa Claus arrives.

"No arrests have been made in the death of the principal of Lincoln School, James Caton, who was found dead at the school a week ago," the local news comes on. "Police have several suspects but have not released their names. An anonymous source has told this station that some of those suspects are employed by the school, and that some teachers are actually afraid to return to work because they fear for their lives if a killer is working among them."

I wrinkle my forehead as I say, "Oh my god, Mother, this is awful." I am in shock about what is said by an anonymous source.

"Who told the news station that there are suspects within the school, and people are afraid for their lives?" Mother's now even more concerned, and I realize the impact that my involvement at the school is having on her.

I raise my voice, "Mother, it had to be Maybelle. She was running around yesterday at our meeting accusing me and accusing Jenny Craig, our social worker. I don't know how many people she has talked to, but I am so fed up with her."

Mother pats me on the shoulder and says, "I know how difficult this is for you."

I continue ranting, "She thinks she can do anything because her husband is on the school board. How dare she talk to the news station! That woman is a snake."

The Macy's Day Thanksgiving Day Parade returns just as we hear voices from the front door.

It's Bud's voice, "Anybody home? Mom, Dana, where are you?"

Then Alex yells, "Hey Grandma, sure smells good in here. Aunt Dana, are you here yet?"

"In the kitchen guys, here we come," Mom answers as we put the dish towels down and go back into the living room to greet Bud and Shelley with hugs, and to take their arms full of food dishes from them.

No hug for Alex, at his age he calls hugs "stupid" like so many other things that fit this description for him. Bud and Shelley follow us back into the kitchen so we can put down the food that Shelley has made. Her vegetable casseroles aren't the best, but we love Shelley, so we tolerate her food.

Alex takes his mom and dad's coats and throws them in the bedroom, "Guys, are you waiting for Santa to come again? That's so babyish." Alex rolls his eyes but focuses intently on the Harry Potter float that is passing by on TV.

"Alex, since you think it's so babyish to watch the parade and wait for Santa, why don't you just go into the bedroom and watch the TV?"

Bud is trying to get Alex out of the way so he can talk to me. I know Bud like the veins on the back of my hand.

From Alex's response, he knows exactly what his dad is trying to do. Alex says, "Sure, Dad, I know, you just want to pound on Aunt Dana to see what she knows about Mr. Cayton's death. I'm sure glad I don't go to that school."

Alex walks out of the kitchen after getting a Mountain Dew out of the refrigerator. Grandma does spoil him with what he likes to eat and drink.

Bud begins his interrogation, "Dana, what's happening? What did the police say to you? What does Ashton know about what's going on?"

Shelley scolds her husband, "Whoa, Bud, lighten up. Dana doesn't want to spend Thanksgiving talking about the mess at school. Let her have some peace."

I answer, "Thanks, Shelley, but it's okay. It's all I can think about, even though I try not to. I was just telling Mom that I have decided to do some informal investigating for myself, and Reba's going to help me."

Bud speaks up, "Holy Shit! Dana, you can't do that. My god there's a murderer loose in our little community, and I don't want you to get hurt. Have the police questioned you?"

I answer Bud's question, "Yes, the police were at school the day after Caton was found and questioned several of us. Unfortunately it looks like I was the last person who saw him before he was found dead. I'm a suspect, at least according to Maybelle, our wonderful school board member's wife."

"Well, I have an interesting new piece of information that I heard yesterday since you brought up Maybelle and her husband," Bud offers.

"Oh my, tell me." I am really curious.

Bud explains, "It seems they've not been making their house payments, and are in danger of having their home foreclosed. Can you believe it? They have that big, beautiful home over on the lake, and they can't even afford it. I always wondered how they could live so high on the hog. They say that house is worth over $500,000 and even though Maybelle's husband is the owner of the concrete company, it would be hard to make those mortgage payments. I also heard that Maybelle buys new designer clothes all the time and will only have the best in her house."

Shelley chimes in, "Dana, I don't see how you can work with Maybelle. She is in my pilates class. You would think she was the teacher the way she tries to take over the class and tell the teacher what to do."

I nod my head yes and say, "That's Maybelle for you. She's always trying to be in control."

Shelley continues, "She'll barely speak to me because I don't wear designer exercise clothes. K-Mart outfits suit me just fine. The other night she was talking about Jenny Craig, isn't she your social worker, and laughing and saying how Jenny should really be in the class because she is so fat."

I say, "Well, that's news to me about the chance that Maybelle and her husband might lose their house. I wonder how they would explain that to everybody."

Just then, the doorbell rings. It has to be Ashton. He doesn't feel quite comfortable enough just to walk in Mother's house. I go to the door and say, "Happy Thanksgiving, Ashton, I'm so glad you could get here."

Ashton hugs me. I need his comfort and strong arms around me. "Hey, Dana, I wouldn't miss your mother's great cooking and your yummy salads. Hope you made your ribbon salad."

"I sure did."

Ashton continues as he sniffs, "Wow. This house smells incredible. I love turkey and dressing. I have to tell you that I may have to leave right after dinner, because we're very close to a breakthrough on the rape case."

Ashton seems a little bothered, but I can tell he doesn't want to give me any details. I have learned not to ask certain things. He will tell me when he can.

I say, "I'm just so glad you could get here for dinner. I know you'll be glad when that case is over."

"Hey, Ashton," says Bud, "good to see you. You look tired pal. I hear you've been working hard on that rape case. If it makes you feel any better, I've heard so many people say they are glad you are handling it. They think you're the man to do the job."

Ashton smiles and says, "Bud, thanks for saying that. I need to hear something positive. I have to tell you that we're getting very close to solving the case, and hope to get a break soon."

Mother comes out from the kitchen to tell all of us to come see Santa, "Come here guys, Santa is just arriving at Macy's. Hey Ashton so glad you're here."

It's truly a great feeling of comfort to me today to be gathered in the kitchen watching the Macy's parade, and putting the finishing touches on Thanksgiving dinner. Even Alex has joined us in the kitchen. He likes hanging out with Ashton. I just have this nagging feeling in my stomach that something could happen to me in this murder case and I don't want these happy moments to end.

As we gather around the table full of wonderful smelling turkey, dressing, salads, Shelley's creamed onions, and my favorite sweet potato casserole, Alex gives our Thanksgiving Prayer, "Thank you dear God, for the many things for which we are grateful, this food, grandma, mom, and dad. Thank you for letting Ashton join us, and thank you for making Aunt Dana such a good teacher. May everyone eat and be as blessed as we are today."

Tears come to my eyes. Leave it to my nephew to point out the positive and make me feel lucky for what I have.

Our dinner features small talk. No one wants to spoil dinner with talk of Cayton or the rape case.

After we've stuffed ourselves and are busy cleaning up, Ashton asks me, "Dana, do you know anything about Mr. Bates' nephew?"

I answer, "I don't know him well but Elliott Bates is a science teacher at the high school. He's been there a couple of years, and everyone is always talking about how good looking he is. Mr. B is so proud of him and all his accomplishments. Last year, he was recognized as the outstanding first year teacher in the district. Do you know him?"

"Not really, I was just wondering," Ashton shrugs.

After cleaning up the kitchen, we gather back at the table and play a game of cards. We have just gotten the cards out, and are complaining about how we ate too much when Ashton's phone rings.

"Ashton here." There is a pause for a short period of time. "Thanks. Great work, I'm on my way."

"Oh, oh, guess no cards for you," I reply, disappointed.

Ashton looks at me, thanks everyone for a great afternoon, and says, "Just got some information. Be sure to watch the six o'clock news."

CHAPTER 12

"Hey guys, let's get the news on," my brother, Bud, comments as we finish our latest card game. It's been a great afternoon with our Thanksgiving dinner, and our traditional afternoon of playing cards, and complaining that we ate too much. We tried not to think about the murder, Ashton's sudden departure after dinner, and his comment to watch the six o'clock news, but our unspoken words communicate that this whole mess is foremost in our mind.

As Bud turns on the TV, and we gather around, Alex is excited, "Hey, is Ashton actually going to be on the news?" His question is answered shortly as the lead in the news comes on.

"Stay tuned for Channel 6 Live at 6 for the latest breaking story on the seventeenth street rape." A picture of Ashton outside the police department flashes across the screen.

My cell phone rings its familiar sound. We're all nervous because we all slightly jump.

I answer it quickly, seeing that it is Reba who refrains from a greeting and gets right to her point, "Quick, turn the news on. I just saw that Ashton is going to be featured."

I respond, "Thanks, Reba, we have it on. Be sure to call me back after the news is off. Ashton didn't say much to us other than there is a big break in the story."

The news commentator comes on, "We're taking you live to the police department where about forty minutes ago, Elliott Bates, a second year teacher at Sunset High School here in Hallicott City has been charged in connection with the reported rape of the minor on seventeenth street." Elliott Bates is seen here being taken into custody. Ashton Gillis, the lead detective in the case, is coming out to make a statement."

I get butterflies in my stomach when Ashton walks outside the police station into the lobby of the municipal building. He takes his place at the podium to read a prepared statement, "This afternoon about 4:15 p.m. Elliott Bates was taken into custody in connection with the alleged rape on 17th Street. Elliott is a teacher at Sunset High School."

Ashton continues, "He is also being questioned in the death of James Caton, the principal at Lincoln School, who was found dead at the school last week. We want to thank everyone who cooperated with our department about this crime. Our sincere regrets go to the victim and her family at this difficult time. We will continue to update this community on further developments." Ashton walks away from the podium.

"Well, what a shock to this quiet community," The female commentator speaks in a quiet shocked tone of voice. "Channel six will keep you posted on further developments as they happen. And now, back to our Thanksgiving Day news."

We are sitting stunned and staring at the TV when Bud speaks up, "My god, do you believe that? A teacher involved in a rape. What is happening to the school system here? First a teacher is arrested for hitting a student. Then a building principal is murdered. Then a teacher rapes a student. Gee, Dana, what is happening to your profession? Maybe you should have gone into business. All this doesn't speak well for the schools, does it?"

I bristle at Bud's comments and respond, "Just because there are some bad apples in the system doesn't mean that all of us are murderers and rapists. Some of us got into this profession to help students learn."

I have gotten sick and tired of everyone criticizing teachers and thinking they can do a better job than we can. Now the latest is they want to abolish tenure and tie our evaluations to the students' test scores. What a time to be in education and all this bad publicity is not going to help those of us who take pride in our work.

Shelley chimes in. "There are a lot of good people in education and you know it, Bud. Dana is a wonderful teacher. You wouldn't want to be criticized if some other insurance agent in town was arrested. This is hard enough on Dana."

Mother questions me. "Dana, did you know that Elliott Bates? Isn't he related to your custodian?"

I answer, "Oh, Mother, that's right, poor Mr. Bates. First he loses his job because he filed a report against Wanda, then he disappears, and now his nephew is arrested. He was so proud of his nephew. He must be devastated."

My cell phone rings again. Reba is checking in. "Do you know anything about the person that Elliott Bates raped? "Do you realize that Elliott is Mr. Bates' nephew? What a mess." Is Ashton coming back to see you tonight?"

I am worked up like Reba is, and respond, "I doubt that Ashton will be back tonight. Sounds like he has a lot of work to do. I wonder who the rape victim could be. What could Elliott have been thinking of?"

Reba responds into the phone, "He's ruined what would have been a promising career."

I answer, "I'll let you know if I hear anything else. I still can't believe this whole thing. I just want to wake up and realize this was just a nightmare. Keep me posted, and

I'll do the same. Try to have a good shopping day tomorrow."

"Stupid," Alex chimes in. "Why would a teacher do something like that?" Just then Alex's cell phone goes off.

Bud and Shelley have allowed Alex to have a cell phone, but he can't have it on during meals and certainly not during the school day. Alex goes in the other room to take his call.

Mother voices her concern, "Oh, Dana, I'm so worried about you. First a murder and now a rape. I thought being a schoolteacher was a safe job for you, but that sure isn't the case here."

I try to reassure her, "I know Mother. Don't worry about me. I'll be fine. I've got to get this whole thing figured out. Ashton said that Elliott is also being questioned in Caton's murder. Why would that be? I don't think that Elliott even knew Caton. Maybe I don't have all the information I need. Wait a minute, maybe Elliott knew Caton through Mr. Bates, since he was our custodian. Now I wonder whether Ashton meant that Elliott may know something about Mr. Bates and his relationship with Caton."

Bud says, "You've lost me, Dana."

I answer, "They might be trying to implicate Mr. Bates from information they can get from Elliott. I better see what Reba thinks about that."

My brother, Bud, must be feeling guilty that he came on pretty strong to me earlier and is trying to redeem himself by offering to help. "Well, I'm having my morning coffee with the guys at the Five Legged Dog in the morning. I'll see what I can find out. Dana, if you're determined to be a detective, I'll keep my ears open."

Shelley speaks up, "While you're out having coffee with the guys, we ladies are going to do our traditional shopping trip, right, Mom and Dana. We have to figure out what time we want to go. Is there anything that you need that's on sale at 4 in the morning?"

Mother says the same thing every year but when we suggest that we can pick her up later she always lets us know that she isn't about to miss anything, "Ugh, do we really want to leave so early in the morning? I need my beauty sleep."

I am eager to get my mind off the craziness in the school system and focus on the craziness of the after thanksgiving shopping so I speak up, "Hey with everything going on we haven't even looked through the newspaper at the ads to see where the real bargains are. Let me get the paper for us."

Mother answers, "Good idea, Dana, why don't you and Shelley look through the newspaper. I'm going to cut us that pumpkin pie that we were all too full to eat at dinner. I think we all need a sugar high."

Shelley says, "Come on Dana, sounds like a plan to me. Alex, you've been on that phone long enough. Come out and help your grandma cut the pie."

I grab the paper and head to the kitchen with Bud, Shelley and Mom.

Bud looks like he is drooling over the pie, "Mom, that pie looks wonderful. Hey Alex, get out here and help. Time's up on the phone."

As Mom is cutting the pie and Shelley and I are leafing through the paper, Alex comes in, and says, "Hey you guys, guess what I just heard."

Bud interrupts, "About time you got out here, what have you been talking about all this time on that phone?"

"You won't believe this." Alex is so excited to tell us his news. "Guess who Elliott Bates raped?"

Shelley comments to her son, "Now, Alex, you don't know who he raped. Ashton just said the name of the victim is not being told because she's a minor."

Alex is eager to finish his story and doesn't want to be doubted by his mother, "Mom, I do know. Elliott Bates had a thing for Michael Flanigan's sister. Michael is in my class, but I don't really hang out with him. But Jeff knows him, and I've been talking to Jeff on the phone just now. Jeff says it was Michael's sister who was raped, but she really wasn't. She and Elliott had been getting it on for quite a while, but her Mother walked in on them and called the police."

I am curious and want to find out what I can from Alex. Kids certainly do know more than the adults sometimes.

I ask, "Wait a minute, Alex, how old is Michael's sister? Is she in college? I thought Ashton said the victim was a minor. I'm confused"

Alex answers pleased with himself that he knows some information that we don't, "Michael's sister is a sophomore at the High School. She's in Mr. Bates science class. She really had a thing for him."

CHAPTER 13

Reba can't believe the news I am sharing over the phone and says, "Denise Flanigan is the rape victim? My God, Dana, I can't believe it. That's Michael's only sister. How did you hear this?"

I call Reba shortly after Alex drops the bomb about who Mr. Bates nephew supposedly raped.

I explain, "Well, it's a long story but seems that Alex got a call from his friend, Jeff, who is a friend also of Michael Flanigan, and Michael let the cat out of the bag that the rape victim was his sister, Denise. According to Alex via Jeff, Denise had a real thing for Elliott and had come on to him, and I got the idea they had been having a fling."

Reba interrupts my non-stop talking, "Oh my goodness, I just can't believe this whole thing."

I continue, "In Alex's terms they were getting it on. Michael's mother walked in and called the police. I still can't believe it. Why would a teacher with such a promising career as Elliott ruin his life by messing around with a high school student?"

Reba answers, "Guess the two of them must have liked rough sex, because Ashton reported that Denise had bruises on her." I don't really know much about the Flanigans. Knowing your nephew, Alex, he'll probably get the whole scoop on the family."

I answer, "Hey Reba, gotten get going. I am trying to get to bed early because we are hitting the stores at four thirty in the morning for Black Friday. I have to be ready to pick Shelley up at four o'clock and mom up at four fifteen to get in line for the five o'clock store opening. We want to get one of those computers for two hundred and seventy nine dollars."

Reba comments, "You are a lot braver than me. I am sleeping in and hitting the stores with my mom no earlier than ten in the morning. I'll connect with you tomorrow. Have a great day."

We're now standing in the mad rush on Friday morning. There are lots of people standing outside the store and more are driving up every minute. I'm thinking about our phone conversation last night and all the happenings on Thanksgiving as we stand in the mad rush on Friday morning.

I say to Mother and Shelley, "I can't believe we are actually standing in this line for a laptop computer at four thirty in the morning. I sure wish I had a little space heater." The cold air and feeling that snow is coming bring me back to reality.

"I sure hope you guys get one," Mother sounds less than hopeful that there will be any computers left when the store opens.

"I hope we do too," adds Shelley. "Bud really wants this laptop, but there ain't no way he'd wait in a line in this cold."

I say, "Well we can't go wrong with a laptop for two hundred seventy nine dollars. What a bargain. I sure need a new one. Mine is so slow. I just hope there are more than twenty since it looks like we are about twenty - third or so in line."

"Brr, it's cold out here," Shelley stamps her feet up and down to keep warm. "It's supposed to snow later. Hey from here are we still planning to head to Kohl's? They've got some great buys on jogging suits, and maybe I should look more fashionable in Pilates to please Maybelle."

I answer, "Kohl's is great with me."

Shelley turns around and looks at the end of the line and asks, "Hey, Dana, isn't that the secretary from your school coming up to get in line?"

I answer Shelley, "It is Andrea Depper. That must be her husband with her. I've never met him before."

Andrea comes up to me and says, "Hey, Dana, good to see you. Looks like we're all a little bit crazy coming out here this early in the freezing cold. Dana, I don't think you've met my husband, Carl. Carl, this is Dana, she teaches fifth grade at my school."

Carl is a short roly poly guy who must like to drink beer from the looks of his belly. Andrea is also short and a bit heavy but somehow, since she is so health conscious, I never expected her to be married to anybody overweight.

Carl replies, "Glad to meet you, Dana, are you in line for one of the computers or are you getting the microwave or mini-frig? We're going for all of them since we're here."

"Just the computer for us." I respond.

Carl laughs, "Hey, Andrea, you can stand here and chat with Dana, I'll go to the end of the line, ha, a school joke for you."

I turn to Andrea and ask, "How are you doing, Andrea, I know it must be hard on you with all that has happened and with you having worked so closely with Caton. Can you believe now that Elliott Bates has been arrested for the rape and he might have also been the killer?"

Andrea responds with a frown on her face, "Oh, Dana, it's rough. I still keep expecting to wake up and realize this is just a big nightmare. I'm so glad we've had these few days off to have some peace and quiet. I hope they get the killer soon, and if it is Elliott, he gets the death penalty. Sorry about that but I feel so strongly that if he is the rapist and killer, he shouldn't get any mercy at all."

I ask "Andrea, maybe you know who brought that cherry pie the other day. I didn't get to taste any of it, but was just curious about who made it."

I am trying to pump her for information about that darn pie. I just can't figure out why it was left out and why there was less of it the day after the murder. Maybe Andrea knows. School secretaries and custodians are really the ones who run the school.

Andrea comments, "Oh, Dana, I'm not sure but I bet Jenny brought it in. You know how she loves to bake and likes to experiment on all of us. Hey, I had better get back there with Carl. Hopefully they'll open the store soon. Have a great day and see you Monday."

We started at Best Buy first before four thirty in the morning, then went to Kohl's, and then the IHOP for breakfast. It's now ten o'clock, and time for our trip to the mall. Shelley and I both got a computer at Best Buy, so we are very pleased. We are patting ourselves on the back that we have survived the herd of elephants who charged into the store when the doors opened.

At Kohl's, Shelley and I tried on the sale jogging suits and each of us get one and I even get one for Maddie for Christmas. She's a small size so it's easy to buy for her. Maddie is one of the other teachers in our building and we always exchange gifts.

"I feel like we've put in a full day already," Shelley says as we get to the mall.

"Me too," I answer.

"I feel like I'm just waking up myself," Mother adds.

The light snow flurries have changed to big beautiful flakes. The whiteness of nature's beauty has changed from tiny white dots of cotton to big white flakes as we make our way quickly from Kohl's to the mall. We step quickly from our car in the crowded parking lot to the door of the mall, Mother and Shelley shake the snow flakes from their coats. My need for the sight of peace causes me to let those white snowflakes sticking to my coat stay there.

"Who's got their list of what we need here?" I ask Shelley and Mom when we get inside the mall entrance.

I really have to change my cell phone ring. There it goes again. The marching music is driving me nuts and right now I have no need for stress.

Sara, my friend who has been substituting for Wanda, calls, "Hi, Dana, hope I'm not interrupting your shopping marathon. We're just getting ready to start ours, and I couldn't wait to share with you what Derek just called about." Derek is Sara's husband and he works with Wanda's husband, Terry, at a big insurance company in town.

Sara continues, "Derek said that Terry came in this morning and told everyone he left Wanda right after she was released from jail. He's filed for divorce from her. He told everybody in the office that he was so sorry for all the embarrassment that his wife's actions have caused, not just at school but in her personal life. He is so sorry she has disgraced herself. He wanted everyone to know that he doesn't condone anything she has done."

I respond, "Oh my, Sara, I really feel sorry for him. He seems like such a nice guy and how Wanda could cheat on him I can't figure it out. What a mess. This whole thing is out of hand, especially now with this and Elliott

Bates being arrested. I have some news for you unless you've already talked to Reba."

Sara responds, "No I was planning to call Reba as soon as I hung up with you. What's up?"

I tell her who the victim was in the rape case, "Well, it seems that Denise Flanigan is a sophomore at Sunset. She supposedly was having a fling with Elliott, and Denise's mother walked in on them, and called the police. My nephew Alex is friends with another kid who knows Michael's sister. Can you believe it?"

Sara gasps, "My God, Dana, I see what you mean. Our community is just falling apart. Well Derek will be interested in hearing this. I'll call Reba and then call him. Listen, Dana, keep me posted. I sure hope nothing else happens for a while."

I answer, "You and me both."

Sara continues, "We're living a soap opera. Can you believe that Elliott is now being questioned in the murder and I wonder whether Mr. Bates will also be questioned? Gotta go."

"Now what's going on Dana?" Mother asks a bit impatiently. She and Shelley have been looking in the store windows while I have been on the phone.

I tell Mom and Shelley what Sara has told me about Wanda's husband leaving her. Mom really doesn't know him but is interested in this latest gossip.

Shelley knows Wanda's husband through Bud and says: "Can you blame him for leaving her? Imagine having an affair with one of your student's parents. That should be grounds enough to fire her, let alone her hitting a student. Now that she's out of jail, will they let her back in the classroom Dana?"

I answer Shelley's question, "Surely not, but I haven't heard what will happen. The union representative

Jessica Flynn, thinks Wanda is just great and took her side in the beginning. Maybe now she will rethink about Wanda being such a wonderful person. Guess I'll hear more about it when I go back to work on Monday. I'm sure not looking forward to that."

By 4:00 we are ready to call it a day and get back to Mom's house so we can reheat the leftovers. Ashton is supposed to come over and join us. Bud and Alex will meet us there to hear all about our shopping escapades.

As we are buying four Christmas ornaments for Mom's buddies, I get a text from Ashton. "Sorry, no dinner for me. Word's out. Bates making claims about Caton blackmailing him.

CHAPTER 14

I relay the latest info to Reba via phone as Mother, Shelley and I are driving back to Mother's after our full day of shopping. "Well, Ashton wasn't supposed to be involved in this murder case but now it's connected to the rape so he's in it whether he wants to be or not. Turns out that Bates was being blackmailed by Caton."

Reba comments, "You can't be serious. I knew Caton was slime but my god he was even worse than I thought. Do you really think Elliott Bates killed Caton?"

I answer, "Reba, I don't know what to think anymore, but now that all this has come out, maybe Maybelle will quit accusing me of the murder."

Reba says, "Hey, gotta go. We sure have a lot to talk about tomorrow. See you at eleven thirty at O'Leary's. Hey, afterwards, I've got a new shop to show you. They sell great colorful clothes and funky jewelry that you'll like."

Reba offers a new shopping option knowing that I never pass up a chance to shop and I love bright color clothes and big pieces of jewelry. Ashton likes to tease me that my necklaces are almost as big as me.

I am excited about spending some fun time with Reba tomorrow, "Sounds like fun. See you at O'Leary's."

One of the most fun parts of Thanksgiving is not just our Turkey Dinner but time to shop and actually have a lunch break.

As we pull in the driveway and hop out of the car, Mother comments as we open the trunk, "Can you believe this trunk is almost completely full of packages? Sure got a lot done."

I respond with a tired voice, but at the same time I am happy and content that we are home. The snow seems to be getting heavier. "We did, Mother, and it was lots of fun."

I don't like driving in the snow but at least it isn't the dreaded ice. We load our arms with the packages, walk very carefully from the driveway to the house, take the packages in the house, kick off our shoes, and dump everything on Mother's bed.

Mother heads to the kitchen to put the leftovers in the oven and Shelley and I set the table. Paper plates are sufficient tonight since the formal turkey day is over.

"Anybody home?" Bud asks as he and Alex come in Mother's house.

"We're in the kitchen," Mother yells out.

Bud directs Alex, "Alex, why don't you go watch TV in Grandma's room?"

"Oh Dad, I know you're just trying to get rid of me so you can talk about the rape and the murder. Guess what I heard today?" Alex responds.

Since Alex had some key information last night we are wondering what his latest bombshell might be.

Shelley looks at her son, "Okay come on, Alex, out with your news."

Alex is so excited and raises his voice, "Well, Mr. Bates has been hangin out with Denise all this year. She loves science and has been sneaking around with him. She told her mother she was staying after school for science club. Her mother believed her, like how dumb is that, and she was hanging out with Mr. Bates after school. You know she already has her driver's license."

Shelley interrupts, "I find this whole thing hard to believe that they didn't get caught earlier."

Alex has a quick response, "Oh, Mrs. Flanigan works and they live close to the school. Mr. Bates was supposed to be helping her with her science project. Ha, some help. Hey, I'm hungry, when are we gonna eat Grandma?"

Mother says, "It'll be about thirty minutes, Alex, have some veggies in the frig to hold you over."

"Ugh, no thanks, I'll go watch TV for awhile." Alex answers disappointed.

Mother anticipates the nightly news, "Speaking of TV, turn ours on. Wonder if anything will be on the news tonight?"

"Ashton didn't say anything about whether he was going to be on TV." I share.

"What a way to become a TV celebrity," Shelley comments, "Ashton is going to get used to TV stardom. Maybe he'll get a promotion at the police department. He deserves it after solving this rape case and now maybe he has solved Caton's murder."

"You know now I'm wondering what kind of car Elliott Bates has?" I am thinking out loud and ask.

"Why do you want to know that?" Bud questions.

I answer, "Remember when I was leaving school the night of the murder, a car went through the parking lot."

Bud questions me, "What color was it? What kind of car?"

"From what I remember it was a white mid-size car. I think it was a Toyota."

Shelley comments, "Dana, that's pretty significant. Have you shared this information with the police?"

I answer, "I sure did, but if that car was Elliott's he's looking even more guilty. That means I probably wasn't the last person to see him. "Bud, did you find out anything today?"

As he pulls a diet coke out of the frig, Bud says, "I sure did and it is quite the scoop. Have you heard that Wanda's husband, Terry, left her?"

Mother smirks as she bursts Bud's bubble, "Oh, that's old news. Dana already got a call about that."

Bud smirks back and gives his Mother a look like I got you, "Well I bet you haven't heard this one? Jason Estes dad was having an affair with Wanda and now Jason's mother has left Jason's dad. She filed for divorce this morning based on adultery and named Wanda in the divorce. Guess the Estes family has quite a bit of money from Mr. Estes' family. Talk today was that Wanda was only really interested in Jason's father for his money."

I interrupt Bud, "Well that figures, Maybelle and Wanda are money hungry, that's for sure. They're gold diggers."

Bud continues, "Seems that Jason's mother is vindictive, not that I blame her, and she's gonna try to take Mr. Estes to the cleaners. They say she is one tough cookie. You know she's a lawyer and is going to get everything she can."

Shelley asks, "How many kids do they have? I just hate to see kids involved in such a messy divorce."

Bud answers, "Jason is their only child and he has to be pretty traumatized by Wanda hitting him. Sure looks like Wanda would have thought twice about hitting a student, especially when his mother is an attorney."

"Wanda deserves everything she gets," I add.

"Shelley opens her mouth in shock," Dana, do you really want to see Wanda get in trouble and lose her job?"

I answer my sister in law, "Shelley, I didn't like Wanda before. She hangs out with Maybelle and they think they run the school and that they are better than the rest of us. She should lose her job. There is no place for teachers who hit students. I'll be interested to see what they decide at her hearing this week."

"Guys, be quiet." Mother tries to shush us up, "Dana, isn't that your janitor walking into the police station?"

"Oh my god, it sure is Mr. Bates." I am stunned.

The news commentator comes on, "We have breaking news about the death of James Caton, principal at Lincoln School. Bob Bates, custodian at Lincoln School and uncle of Elliott Bates, who is in custody for the rape on Seventeenth Street, is now being questioned in the murder of James Caton. Bob Bates was suspended from his job the day Caton was murdered."

CHAPTER 15

My cell phone sounds off. I answer. It's Ashton, "Hey, Dana, Sorry. I've been wrapped up in this case and haven't gotten to talk much. I really wanted to join you last night at your mother's. Thought I better give you a heads up. The department may need to question you later today. We're expecting the autopsy and toxicology reports."

I look at my clock beside the bed, and it shows 8:15.

I reply as I yawn, "Oh, Ashton, it's so good to have you wake me up. Wish you could be here in person."

"What have you got going today?"

"Reba and I are having lunch at O'Leary's and then doing some shopping."

"Sounds like fun."

I pause, "Hey, Ashton, why might I get called in today? Am I in trouble again? I thought Elliott Bates and poor Mr. Bates were the big suspects. What have I done now?"

Ashton says in a low voice as he tries to calm me, "Two things you told the police, the white car and the cherry pie, may be significant. We need to ask you a few more questions. I know this whole thing is hard on you, and I wish I could give you more support. I don't like being involved in this case, but since it looks like the rape and murder are related, I'm involved whether I like it or not."

I don't want to upset Ashton because I know he has a lot on his mind, "Don't worry, I'll be okay."

Ashton says, "I gotta run. Dana, you're my best."

"And you're my best. See you tonight."

Ashton and I refer to each other as our best boyfriend and girlfriend. We have dated exclusively for almost two years. We know we have deep feelings for each other, but both of us were burned in past relationships and are afraid to talk love and lifetime commitment. That a-hole I dated and was engaged to dumped me for somebody else. Ashton's ex girlfriend, who was a business executive, decided she didn't want to marry "a beat cop."

I look at the time and decide to go ahead, get up, and get ready leisurely before meeting Reba at 11:30. Reba is my best friend and is happily married to Barry. She is eager for me to settle down to a married life. She knows I care deeply for Ashton, but is afraid I will end up an old maid. I am 39 and never married. I know Ashton's a good thing, but I'm so scared to make a permanent commitment.

I look around the condo and think I had better do a little cleaning before I get my shower. I love my condo with its light vanilla ice cream color carpet and furniture. Because I love bright colors I have bright yellow and orange pillows and throws on the furniture. My kitchen has hardwood floors and is done in yellow and orange. With my wicker table and chairs this is truly home for me.

I fix a quick cup of coffee with the coffee maker Ashton bought me. I get out my usual granola, and have a bowl with some yogurt. I put my packages from yesterday's shopping spree away in my spare bedroom until I get some time to wrap them. I do a quick bathroom clean and get out the vacuum to give the condo a good dusting.

I've had enough cleaning for one day. I head for the shower. Today I'm in the mood for my black jeans and jacket and my bright yellow turtleneck. The snow stopped late last night and a look out my condo tells me that they have cleaned off the streets. But the sidewalks still look slick. I pull out my black suede boots and put them on.

Traffic is probably bad today so I want to leave early to give myself plenty of time to get to O'Leary's for lunch. I love their fresh salads.

As I get in the car, crank up the heater and pull out of the small garage below my condo, I turn on the radio to see if there is any news I have missed. The oldies but goodies station is playing Christmas music to get us in the mood for lots of Christmas shopping, hoping that this will stimulate our floundering economy.

As I turn in the parking lot of O'Leary's, the 11:30 news comes on. I don't see Reba's car in the lot, so I decide to sit in the car and listen to the news until she gets here.

The newscaster announces, "The murder of James Caton leads this local newscast. Elliott Bates, a teacher at Sunset High School, has been arrested in the rape over on Seventeenth Street, and is now a suspect in James Caton's murder. Sources say Caton may have been blackmailing Bates. Robert Bates, the uncle of Elliott Bates and a custodian at Caton's school, was brought in for questioning last night, but was released later in the evening. The senior Bates had been suspended by Caton earlier the day that Caton's body was found. We'll bring you up to date reports on this rape and murder that have shocked our fine community."

I decide to go ahead in and get a table. I hope Reba gets here soon. We've got a lot to discuss.

As I walk in the door, I see Reba waving her hand from one of the tables.

When I get close, Reba says, "Hey, Dana, what's up? I was getting worried when you were late."

"Sorry about that, but the eleven thirty news came on, and I wanted to hear it. I didn't see your car in the lot."

"Barry dropped me off," Reba says. "Hope you don't mind driving us to that new little boutique and taking me home after. You know I hate to drive in snow."

"No problem but you should've called. I would have picked you up, and saved Barry a trip."

Reba waves a hand in dismissal. "Barry was going in to his office anyway, so it was on his way. Tell me what was on the news?"

I shrug, "They said Mr. B was released last night after he was questioned. The radio made it sound like poor Mr. B. did something wrong and was suspended. Caton really hurt a lot of people."

"And still is from his grave. Oops, guess he isn't in his grave yet."

I smile, "Ashton called me this morning and said the autopsy report may be available later today, and the news just said the same thing. Ashton also said I might be questioned later."

"Why, you've already talked to them?"

I answer, "Remember I saw the white car pull in and out of the parking lot. I also raised the issue with the cherry pie that I know I put in the frig the night of the murder, and it was out with another piece missing the next day."

The waitress approaches our table to take our drink order, "What can I get you lovely ladies today?"

As the waitress leaves, I add, "I know two things I'm not eating today. Turkey and cherry pie. I still wonder what happened to that darn pie. By the way, I saw Andrea Depper while we were in line waiting for the computer. Her husband is kind of dorky. He was trying to make a joke that wasn't really funny about going to the back of the line. You know, like we send kids to the back of the line."

Reba grins, "I've heard he's a little weird."

"Anyway, I asked her who she thought made the pie because I never heard, and I figure as the school secretary she knows a lot. She said it was Jenny."

"That makes sense. You know how Jenny loves to cook and bake. Why do you think that's important?"

I shake my head, "I don't know, but it has to be. Somebody had to come back in the building and eat another piece of pie, or Caton had to come down from his pedestal to enter the teacher's lounge, and eat the piece of pie and left it out. My gut says the pie and the white car are part of the murder mystery."

Reba leans forward, "Dana, did the car actually stop in the parking lot, or did it just go through?"

"It was just going through and maybe somebody was just turning around." I have thought about that night so many times and keep trying to put the puzzle together.

"Maybe the car was pulling in," Reba offers, "and when it saw you were getting ready to pull out of the lot left and came back later."

The waitress returns to take our food order. "I have to tell you that the people over at that corner table are convinced you two are teachers where that school principal was murdered. Hey, if you are, aren't you scared to go back to work there?"

Reba answers quickly, "Yes, we teach at Lincoln School, and no, we're not scared. We're teachers. We're not scared of anybody. I'm going to have the cobb salad with blue cheese dressing on it."

I add, "I'd like the O'Leary's salad with chicken and your house dressing."

As the waitress walks away, Reba says, "Don't look but those two ladies are staring at us. I guess we're all going to be famous or infamous."

"Reba, I think those two ladies are in Mother's Silver Sneakers exercise classes." I look over and wave.

Reba grabs my forearm, "Now back to the case we have to solve. Who owns a white car that you said was probably a Toyota Camry?"

I answer a little too loudly, "I don't have a clue, but let's do some exploring and see what we can come up with. We've got to get some answers."

I look around the dining room, "What do you think will happen to Wanda?"

"She has a hearing on Tuesday night with the school board and who knows what will happen," Reba responds, "With Maybelle's husband on the school board and the union president, Jessica, on her side she may return to class, but surely they will take Jason out of her class."

"I sure hope she never sees the inside of a classroom again."

We finish our lunch and pay our bills.

"Hey let's get out of here," Reba says, "I want to show you that new shop. Get your credit card ready."

We head to the car to get to Bev's Boutique.

On our way, my marching music phone goes off. I answer, "Hey Sara, what's up? We just had lunch at O'Leary's and are headed to the new boutique. Want to meet us there?" Sara is a friend who is subbing in our school for Wanda.

I listen to what Sara is saying while Reba is asking in the background, "What's happening?"

I respond to Sara, "Ashton said they might have an autopsy report. What did you hear?"

I listen to Sara's reply. I am stunned. "Oh my God, Sara, I don't believe it. See you in a little while. You have to help Reba and I solve this case." I hang up the phone.

"What did Sara say that has your face as white as the whiteboard in my class?"

I answer softly, "Caton was poisoned."

CHAPTER 16

"Did you know that Caton was allergic to fish oil?" I say to Reba, still in disbelief after Sara has told us that Caton's body had fish oil in it, and that's what killed him.

As we pull into the small parking lot at Bev's Boutique, both of us are still stunned and just sit in the car trying to pull our thoughts together.

Reva's mind wanders back to our annual potluck at the beginning of the school year and she says, "I didn't know much about Caton other than he was the world's worst principal. Now that you mention it remember at our opening potluck, Jenny brought that yummy seafood salad that everybody raved about."

As I answer, I think of how wonderful it not only tasted but smelled. "You're right. It was so good. I could have eaten the whole bowl. Jenny told me that she had asked Caton if he had tried it. He was very abrupt and said 'no and I don't intend to."

"Poor Jenny was so hurt," Reba recalls.

I can smell the unpleasant odor of fish oil as I answer, "Where do you think he got fish oil? I take fish oil every day because it's so good for you, but if he was allergic to it he sure wouldn't have taken any unless he was trying to kill himself and somehow I can't imagine that. He was stuck on himself. So how did he get it?"

Reba's phone rings and she answers, "Hi, doll, what's up? We're just sitting outside the new boutique. Wait til you hear the latest news."

Reba pauses as she listens to what Barry, her husband, has to say.

Reba says, "Oh my God, Dana knew there was something up in that pie but how could that happen.

How did fish oil get into the cherry pie? Andrea Depper told Dana that Jenny made that pie."

Reba listens as her husband tells her what he has learned through his attorney's network.

"We should be home in a couple of hours. Sara is meeting us here."

Reba puts the phone back in her purse, "Dana, your hunch about something being wrong with the pie may be right. Seems that cherry pie and fish oil were found in Caton's body and he died from an allergic reaction to the fish oil. Barry heard now they are separately testing that cherry pie to see if the fish oil was in it."

I ask, "Did you eat any of the pie? Wouldn't the pie taste like fish oil if the oil was in it."

"I didn't eat any but didn't you say that half of it was left so not too many people tried it," Reba recalls.

"Half of it was left when I put it back in the frig but then another piece was gone when I saw it out the next morning," I answer.

I can still see that pie sitting out the next morning after I know I put it back in the refrigerator the night before.

"They'll also know whose fingerprints were on the pie," Reba offers.

"Wait a minute, Reba, my fingerprints are on that pie. This isn't looking good for me."

"Now, let's think about this, Dana. There are two possibilities. Either the fish oil was in the pie all along, or it was added later after half of it was gone when somebody knew that Caton might eat a piece of it."

"Good point, Reba, that makes perfect sense."

Reba continues, "Maybe somebody even served Caton a piece of the pie. Then your fingerprints won't mean anything."

"You might be right about me, but this sure isn't looking good for Jenny. Maybelle has sure pointed out to everybody that Jenny hated Caton."

We had been sitting in the car trying to figure out what happened when we hear a horn and look up to see Sara pulling into the lot.

Count on Reba to steer the conversation back to shopping, her favorite hobby, "Let's get out. We need to look at some bright cheery clothes and jewelry. Maybe Bev's Boutique will cheer us up."

I say, "I still hope that I'm in the clear. I don't like it that my fingerprints were on the pie. That'll teach me to be a neat freak and put the pie away. Wish I would've just left it out."

Sara jumps out of her car, and comes over to greet us as we are getting out of my car. She is so energetic and bubbly. "Can you believe this whole thing?"

We then fill Sara in with the information we got after she called us to tell us that Caton was poisoned with fish oil. She hasn't heard about the cherry pie as a possible source for the fish oil.

Sara sounds shocked, "The cherry pie? Oh no, if it's true and Jenny did make the pie she's in deep do-do. I wasn't subbing that day so I don't know much about the pie."

Reba has the shopping bug. "Why don't we get our minds off this for awhile and enjoy the boutique. Then let's start making some calls to some of the staff, Maybelle and Wanda excluded, to see if anybody ate the cherry pie during the day."

Sara adds, "I wouldn't put it past either one of them to have laced the pie with fish oil. Yuck, that sounds awful. I'm with you Reba, let's do some shopping and then get to sleuthing."

As we enter the boutique, I have an adrenaline rush as I see all the beautiful bright colors. With winter coming, I need bright to remind me that spring will come next. Reba was right. These are my kind of clothes. Lime greens, yellows, oranges. You would think we were in sunny Florida rather than here in cold Hallicott City, Illinois.

The boutique is pretty crowded. The owner, Bev, is mingling and helping people as needed. We approach her and introduce ourselves.

Bev comments, "My cousin works in that school. I feel so sorry for you guys. Her name is Jenny Craig. She's the social worker. Do you know her?"

Reba recalls all the yummy dishes that Jenny has made for us, including the seafood salad, but she doesn't mention cherry pie." Of course we do. We love Jenny. She is a great social worker, and a great cook."

"You bet she is," says Bev. "Her pies and salads are to die for. She made five pies for Thanksgiving at Grandma's house. None of us even try to compete with her. She makes all the pies for our family."

We must look funny because Bev asks, "Is everything all right with you? You look concerned."

Reba responds, "Everything is just fine. We're just worried that a couple of the other teachers haven't been very nice to her."

"Oh, you mean Maybelle and Wanda," Bev whispers, "I know all about them, and the games they play. Can you believe that Wanda and what she did?"

Just then we hear a customer comment, "Bev, can you help me over here?"

Bev moves away from us. "Sure just a minute. Excuse me ladies, feel free to browse and let me know if you need anything,"

"This was sure an expensive stop for me," I comment as we're leaving the boutique an hour and a half later with bags in hand.

Sara is excited and feeling a shopping high. "Oh, Dana, I love those two jackets you bought, and the yellow earrings will go with either jacket." "I went in there just to look and I couldn't resist those slacks and the matching sweater."

Reba adds, "I can't gain any weight since that dress fits me perfectly now. I needed a red dress for the holidays." Reba's favorite color is red.

Sara says her goodbye, "I gotta go. This was so much fun, thanks for inviting me to meet you. Call me with any news. I'll do the same."

My phone goes off. I answer and recognize Jenny's voice right away, and she is clearly distressed. "I called Bev and she said you had just left the boutique so I thought I'd catch you. I don't know what to do."

"What do you mean? Is everything okay?"

"No it's awful. The police just called and told me to come there right away. They say that Caton was poisoned by my cherry pie."

CHAPTER 17

"Did you tell the police I made the pie?" Jenny is clearly upset and seems mad at me thinking I am the squealer. Our phone conversation sure has started wrong.

I am so disappointed that Jenny seems to think that I am against her. I'm certainly on her side. "Jenny, I sure didn't. Andrea Depper told me you made the pie. I ran into her Friday morning at the big sales."

Poor Jenny is distraught at the thought that someone would tamper with her pie. "Sure I made the pie, but I didn't poison Caton. I hated him but I wouldn't kill him. The police said somebody put fish oil in my pie, and it killed Caton. I didn't even know he was allergic to fish oil, and besides I wouldn't make a cherry pie with fish oil. Yuck."

I am realizing that Jenny is in a lot of hot water and better not be interviewed by the police alone. "Of course you wouldn't. We know you wouldn't kill Caton. What are you going to do? Do you think you better get a lawyer?"

Jenny has a plan, but it hinges on Jessica being available, and says, "I don't know what to do. I'm going to try to get hold of Jessica, the union representative. The union should help me."

I am frightened for Jenny because she can be so naïve sometimes. "Jenny, call her right away, and then call me back. In the meantime, I'm going to have Reba ask Barry what you should do. Even though Barry isn't an attorney who handles criminal cases, he can probably give us some advice."

Jenny has clearly been insulted by my reference to criminal cases, but that's what this is. She raises her voice and says, "I'm not a criminal, Dana. This is terrible."

"Jenny, I didn't mean that you were a criminal but this is a criminal case because, face it, Caton was murdered."

Panic is clear in Jenny's voice. "Dana, I know you didn't mean to insult me. It's just I am beside myself. What if they arrest me? What will I do?"

"Jenny, calm down, we'll help you. Reba and I are going to solve this case. Call Jessica right now."

Reba's mouth is hanging open as Reba is hearing only my side of the phone conversation. "What has happened now. What do you want me to ask Barry?"

My mind is racing as I answer Reba's question. "Jenny has to go down to the police station. She's being questioned in the murder, and frankly it sure doesn't look good for her, Reba. The question I have is whether she should go down there alone, or should she get an attorney? She is calling Jessica, but is that enough, and what if Jessica isn't available."

Reba's punching the buttons on her phone calling her husband, Barry, "Hi, doll, you remember Jenny Craig, our social worker. Long story short is that Caton was poisoned by fish oil that was in the cherry pie that Jenny made, and the police have called her. They told her to come in for questioning."

Reba pauses as Barry must be asking questions.

She continues, "We told her to get hold of the union representative right away, because we don't think she should be questioned without a lawyer present. This sure doesn't look good for her. We told her to call us right back about whether she could get hold of Jessica."

Reba stops talking again to listen to what Barry is saying. "Great. I'll call you back as soon as we hear from Jenny. Thanks."

"My curiosity is killing me. Tell me what Barry said. I'm wondering whether we should go down to the police station with Jenny. I feel so sorry for her. She's our social worker and always helping others, and now she needs our help."

Reba answers me with a scowl on her face. "Barry said she should definitely call the union folks because she's supposed to be represented by them. However, he said that if they won't come to her rescue today, she should go ahead and talk to the police because she has nothing to hide if she didn't do it. However, heaven forbid if they arrest her tonight and the union still doesn't come through, then she'll have to hire a private attorney. Barry is going to make a couple of calls just in case."

"Thank god for Barry," I say.

"He knows a good criminal attorney but doesn't know whether he will want to get involved in this case."

I respond, "Sounds like we have a plan. Now let's hope we hear from Jenny pretty soon. Why don't we head over to her house? Sounds like she needs some friends right now."

"Good idea," Reba agrees.

It has started snowing again, and I feel a bit anxious and would like to get home but Jenny needs us.

"I'll call Jenny and tell her we're on the way."

We have been so preoccupied that we didn't realize we've been sitting in Bev's boutique parking lot all this time. As we head out of the lot, I keep thinking about the white car in the parking lot and what the connection could be. I know the car doesn't belong to Jenny. She drives a red Chrysler Sebring so it wasn't her circling around in the parking lot. Who could it be?

The phone brings me out of my daydreaming. On the other end I hear Ashton's voice.

He's reminding me of our date, "Dana, how's it going? Hope you've had a great day. Will you be home later this evening? Just remembered that we have a dinner date at seven tonight, and I think I might actually make it."

"Believe me, Ashton, I haven't forgotten about tonight. Can't wait."

Ashton continues, "It's been a crazy day here so I'm ready to spend some time unwinding."

I had thought that he would probably have to cancel so I am thrilled that we can get together for an evening. This whole vacation I have only seen him briefly at Thanksgiving.

Ashton continues, "Where are you now? Hope you had a great day with Reba."

"Reba and I had a great lunch and did some financial damage at Bev's Boutique. Seven is fine for me. I'm going to be so glad to see you. Poor Jenny. We're so upset about her being accused of poisoning Caton. We're headed over to her house right now to comfort her before she goes to the police station."

Ashton cautions me, "Dana, let's be precise. She hasn't really been accused yet of poisoning Caton, but we want to question her because she made the cherry pie with fish oil in it."

"But that's just it, Ashton, she didn't put any fish oil in the pie. Somebody else had to have done it."

"Well if you are headed over there, tell her she needs to get here by five o'clock. We told her that but she started crying, so I'm not so sure what actually registered with her."

"Will do, Ashton, see you at seven. Where are we going?"

"It's a surprise. See you then, and, Dana, be careful, the roads are getting slick."

Reba is dying for more information, "Ooh, hot date tonight with Ashton? About time. With all this stuff going on you haven't gotten to see him much. I can't wait to hear what he said to you."

"Ashton said that Jenny is supposed to be down at the police station by five p.m. I hope we can get her calmed down, and she has gotten hold of the union by now. Funny she hasn't called us."

As I turn on to Jenny's street, the phone rings. It's Jenny.

"Dana, I'm sorry I haven't called back, but I got hold of Jessica, She says she'll try to get hold of the union attorney so he can go with me. I'm so nervous. This makes going to the doctor's office look like a piece of cake."

"Jenny, we're just coming down the street. We figured you needed some emotional support until you go to the police station, so we'll be there in a minute."

"Wonderful. I'll get a pot of decaf started, and I baked some cookies earlier today."

Leave it to Jenny to always have fresh baked goods on hand, although I'm thinking that her baking reputation sure isn't to her advantage right now.

Jenny is at the door as we pull in the driveway, hop out, and greet her with hugs. We take our boots off not wanting to bring snow in on her hardwood floors. Jenny bought this little bungalow about four years ago, and she remodeled the whole thing. It is so warm and cozy. She has the fake fireplace in the living room on, so it feels incredible on such a blustery day. I figure I had better check on what time she is supposed to go to the police station because it is 3:30 now.

"Jenny, what time do you have to be down at the police station?"

"They told me I had to be there by 5 so I'm hoping I hear back from Jessica. Sit down and give me a minute to get your coffee and the cookies. I know you both like your coffee black."

Jenny has such great attention to detail that I was surprised she didn't know that Caton was allergic to fish oil. Or did she and she didn't want to tell us?

The aroma from the kitchen is wonderful. We can tell she baked those chocolate chip cookies today. Nothing like the smell of chocolate chips to relax us, but it doesn't seem to be working for Jenny who is very edgy, and rightfully so.

Reba relays what Barry told us about the game plan if the union attorney can't go with her downtown when she is questioned by the police.

Jenny returns with our coffee and a tray of those scrumptious smelling cookies. Both Reba and I go for one immediately.

Jenny says, "It sounds like a good plan to me. I had also decided that if the union attorney couldn't go with me, I was going alone, but I'm scared. What if the news gets me on camera and I'm on the news tonight as a suspect. I'll never be able to show my face again at school. The students will have no respect for me. After all, they'll see me as a possible murderer."

"Now, Jenny, let's not think the worst." I lower my voice in an effort to calm Jenny.

"My god, I'm so scared, and I don't think I will ever bring any more food in to school at all. And how am I ever going to face that horrible Maybelle?"

I try to reassure her, "Jenny, it's going to be okay. No one thinks you're a murderer."

As I say it I am thinking that it doesn't look good for her. Then again, I keep remembering I'm a suspect too.

Jenny's cell phone rings. Hopefully this is Jessica with some good news. I hope Jessica is going to help Jenny. Her job as union representative is to represent the members, not be partial to Wanda and Maybelle.

Jenny is listening intently and then we hear her say, "I'll meet her there at four thirty. Thanks so much, Jessica, I really appreciate this."

Jenny turns to us and says, "Okay, that makes me feel better. Pat Glascoe, the union attorney....remember she was there when some people were interrogated before....is going to meet me at the police department promptly at 4:30. What a relief. I'm still petrified, but at least I won't be alone. Thanks, guys, for giving me the advice. I don't know what I would have done. I was in a panic."

As Reba finishes up her last sip of coffee and takes the last bite of her second chocolate chip cookie, she says, "Now that I've gained another couple of pounds from these cookies, we better get out of here so you can get ready to go. Barry is expecting me by 4:30 too. Good luck, Jenny, let us know how it goes."

Reba and I walk carefully to the car because the snow is sticking, and Jenny's driveway is a bit slick. I shut the door of the car as I say, "Brrr, it's getting cold out here. I sure hope everything goes okay for Jenny. What a rough situation she's in." I turn the heater on full blast.

Reba answers, "You're right. It doesn't look good for her."

"I thought things were bad for me but they aren't looking very good for her either. Can you imagine! Somebody had to put fish oil in her pie."

Reba changes the subject, "Dana, I've been thinking about Mrs. Caton. We haven't heard anything about her and her reaction to all that's happening, and there hasn't been any word on a Memorial Service. I didn't like Caton, but I feel sorry for his wife and kids."

"You're right, Reba, we haven't gotten any news about the memorial service. I feel bad for her too."

Reba continues as she raises an issue that has been on my mind. "After all, not only was she married to a jerk but he was killed. Do you think if we could talk to her she might shed some light on who else hated him enough to kill him?"

"Reba, I'm wondering that myself. Do you think we should make a visit to Mrs. Caton to express our condolences? I don't think they live too far from here, do they? Oops, I mean she doesn't live too far from here."

Reba answers, "If you're going to get me home by four thirty, maybe we should just drive by and see if there are any people there. Then after school on Monday we can go over and take her some flowers."

"Good idea, I want to get home and get ready for my night out with Ashton. I am so looking forward to this evening."

"Do you remember the address, or I can google it?" Reba has her phone out ready to google.

"I remember Jenny said it's only about three blocks from her house and it's on Sunset, but I'm not sure of the exact address. Let's definitely drive by. Google it and see what you get."

I have mixed feelings. I want to do some sleuthing but also want to get home and get ready for my date.

"Here it is. James Caton, 33 Sunset Drive." Reba puts her phone back in her purse.

"I think Sunset is just two streets over so let me find it." I have a vague recollection of where the street is. I think that Ashton got called out for a domestic violence situation on that street, and he said it was nice neighborhood.

"Here is Sunset, now the address is 33 Sunset. Ooh, these are some nice homes. Caton was making good money in the school system, even though he sure didn't earn it. Can you see any numbers on the houses?"

"There it is, Dana, that red brick house with the boat on the side of the yard. He even had a boat."

The realization of what I am now seeing besides the boat is overwhelming, and I feel my heart racing.

"Pull off to the side, Dana, do you see what I see?"

"That white car, that's it, the one that was pulling out of the parking lot that night. Reba, I know that's the car."

I glare at the car.

Reba is talking fast, "Wait a minute. We don't know whether that belongs to Caton or his wife, or somebody is visiting. There is only one way to find out."

I am stunned by what I am seeing and say excitedly to Reba, "What are we going to do?"

Reba already has a plan in mind. "We're going to go up to the door and give our condolences, and ask about the car."

I want to get some answers about the white car. "Good idea, how about if I just happened to have noticed that one of the tire's air looks low, and ask if the car is hers? Let's go. That is definitely the same car that went through the parking lot."

We are walking cautiously as we get out of the car and make our way up the driveway because it is getting even slicker than when we left Jenny's. We ring the doorbell and the porch light comes on, even though it isn't dark. We see two kids peeking out the front window. A short petite woman opens the main door but doesn't open the storm door and looks at us and talks through the door. After her husband has been murdered, it figures she wouldn't open the door for us. "Can I help you?"

Reba takes the lead. "Mrs. Caton, we are teachers at Lincoln School, and just came by to tell you how sorry we are about your husband, and if there is anything we can do, just let us know."

"Thank you for coming by, but I'm really not up to talking with anyone right now."

I respond, "We understand and we'll see you at the memorial service. We just wanted to stop by. I take a step back and pause: "Mrs. Caton, is that your car, or do you have company? It looks like the back right tire is very low, so please do check it."

"Yes, that's my car, and I don't have room for it in the garage right now, so have been leaving it out. I'll get the tire checked tomorrow. Thanks."

CHAPTER 18

"Are you sure that's the same car that was pulling out of the parking lot?" Reba questions me.

"I'm 99 percent sure it had to be the car, and why was she circling the school parking lot? Why didn't she just pull in and see her husband?"

Reba answers, "She probably didn't want her husband to know she was checking on him. She must have been checking to see what he was up to. What did she think he was doing?"

I add, "I'm definitely going to tell Ashton tonight. This may be significant information."

My mind races after seeing that the white car I saw turning around belonged to Mrs. Caton.

Reba changes the topic from Mrs. Caton. "Before we get back to my house, let's call Maddie and see if she ate any of the cherry pie. You know how Maddie loves sweets. She and Chris should be home by now."

"I don't think I heard when they were coming home."

Reba knows the answer, "They were going to his parents for Thanksgiving, but coming back today so they can spend tomorrow with her parents."

Reba can remember everybody's schedule. Maddie is our good friend who teaches fourth grade. She has only been married two years and she and her husband, Chris, are still trying to keep both sides of the family happy.

Reba is pressing the buttons on her cell, "I'll try to get her now."

"Hey, Maddie, how was your weekend?"

There is a long pause as Reba listens to Maddie's Thanksgiving update. "Did you happen to eat a piece of the cherry pie that was in the lounge the day Caton died?"

Reba is nodding her head up and down to let me know what Maddie says as she responds to her, "Maddie, did the pie taste strange? Are you sure?"

Maddie must be saying that it tasted good.

"We heard Jenny made it and I know she's a great cook," Reba is silent again then explains to Maddie that Jenny is down at the police station and tells the details of what has led up to the event.

"Thanks, Maddie, we'll keep you posted and see you Monday. Not looking forward to it but guess we have no choice to go back. See you."

Reba relays her conversation to me, "Maddie says she ate a big piece for her dessert at lunch time and she thinks that Maybelle ate a piece and Andrea Depper ate some. When you ran into Andrea, did she say she ate a piece?"

"No, she didn't say she had any. When I asked her about the pie she told me that Jenny made it. That's strange."

"Wonder why she didn't say she had a piece. I'm surprised Maybelle would have a piece, since she hates Jenny. Probably didn't know Jenny made it."

I guess now we know that the pie was okay during part of the day. That means that someone had to add the fish oil sometime after lunch. I better tell Ashton about this because it shows that Jenny didn't put the fish oil in when she made the pie."

Reba asks in a doubting tone, "This doesn't get Jenny off the hook because the police could still think that Jenny added the fish oil later. Wait a minute; maybe you can't taste the fish oil when it's cooked. Was Jenny at school all day? Wonder when she left school?"

"I don't remember. I was so upset about reporting Wanda's behavior to the Department of Children and Family Services, and then getting called in to see Caton. Wait a minute; I didn't see Jenny in the afternoon at all."

Reba adds, "I didn't either, now that you say that."

I answer, "We need to ask her if she was out of the building because that could help clear her from being the suspect. I'll try to call her later to see how her police interrogation went and I'll ask her or maybe Ashton will tell me what happened."

I am thinking I will try to reach her before Ashton gets to my condo for our date.

We pull in Reba's driveway. Reba invites me in for a quick drink, but I have to decline. "Thanks, Reba, but I want to get home and get ready for my date with Ashton. I'm so excited about spending time with him tonight. Hope we can just relax and enjoy our evening."

"Enjoy your date. I'll talk to you tomorrow. Don't worry, I won't call too early. Bet you'll be tired after tonight. Make up for the lost time."

Reba gets out of the car and heads toward her front door. I drive home thinking about all the information I've gotten today. I can't wait to share it with Ashton. I pull my car in the underground parking garage of my condo building. I'm really glad that I have inside parking because the weather keeps getting nastier. I feel a chill as I open the car door, get my packages out of the trunk and walk to the elevator to go up to my condo.

I glance at my cellphone and see it's almost six. I better hustle if I'm going to get ready and get some wine chilled by the time Ashton gets here at 7. As I unlock my door, I flip on the lights, and admit I'm glad to be home.

My condo gives me a sense of security. I put my sacks in a corner of the bedroom and make sure the room looks comfy as I hope Ashton will spend the night. I go out to the kitchen, flip the light on, and get out a bottle of wine. I fill the ice bucket with ice and put in the wine bottle. I make my way back to the bedroom and get out of my clothes and into the shower, I hear the phone ring. Darn. It'll have to wait.

I've taken my quick shower and wrapped my warm robe around me. I look at the phone. Ashton called and left a message. "Can't wait until I see you. I'm running a little late, probably about a half hour, but will be there. Tell you all about it."

At least that gives me a little more time to get dressed and beautified for Ashton. Since I don't know where we're going I decide on my nice grey slacks and a pink turtleneck.

When Ashton walks in the door, I greet him with a big hug and kiss. I'm so glad to see his smiling, yet tired, looking face.

"Ashton, am I glad to see you. Seems like an age."

We linger in our embrace and kiss.

As we catch our breath, I say, "Hey, I've got some new Riesling chilling. Ready for some? You're not on duty are you?"

Ashton looks at me with his sexy eyes. When he licks his lips, I know what that means for later in the evening.

"Dana, I most certainly am off duty, and can we just skip dinner for now and escape to a better place."

Ashton leads me into the bedroom, and he and I release all the pent up tension of this week. The yearning for him overtakes me, and we quickly undress each other and collapse on the bed.

Two hours later, feeling such a sense of peace and contentment, I ask Ashton if he is ready for the glass of Reisling.

"I'd rather hop in the shower, and then have the wine and dinner. Come join me."

"Delighted to." I say as Ashton takes me by the hands and leads me into the bathroom.

That shower leads to more lovemaking both in and out of the shower.

"Maybe now that Riesling would be good," Ashley says as he slips his pants back on and I throw a robe on.

Ashton proposes a toast as we sit together in the living room with our wine, "To my fellow detective, and the best and only love I have."

"I'll certainly drink to that. You don't know what the last four hours have meant to me. Ashton, I've missed you so much and wish we could just stay like this until all this junk passes over."

Ashton raises his glass as he says, "I'll drink to that. Dana, what do you want to do for the dinner? Now I have an appetite and I feel bad that I didn't take you out to dinner. Guess we could still go out to one of our all-night diners."

"I vote for staying in. I have some eggs and I can whip up a mean cheese omelet. How does that sound?"

"Works for me, Dana, you're my best. After the omelet, maybe we can relieve some more stress."

I say, "Come in the kitchen and keep me company and tell me about your last few days. I have news to share with you too."

Ashton answers, "You know we questioned Jenny this afternoon and her cherry pie is what poisoned Caton. It was full of fish oil and apparently Caton had a bad allergy to fish oil."

I explain to Ashton that Jenny did make the pie. Reba and I had asked Maddie whether she had a piece of the pie, and Maddie said she didn't taste anything unusual and that could mean that someone else put the fish oil in the pie later.

"Supposedly Andrea Depper, our school secretary, also had a piece of the pie. You need to know that Jenny may have been out of the building in the afternoon so she may not have even been around the pie."

Ashton answers, "Jenny said she was out on a home visit in the afternoon and we are going to verify whether that is true. She still could have come back later and put fish oil in the pie and we are also trying to figure out whether you could taste fish oil if she baked it in the pie. This whole thing is bizarre. How many people do you think really knew that Caton was allergic to fish oil?"

"Not many did, but I suspect that Andrea knew. The school secretary always knows everything."

"Thanks, Dana. We'll probably question her again and guess we better question Maddie now that I know she ate part of the pie. We have released Jenny, but she was told she can't leave town."

As I beat the eggs, cheese, and spices for our omelet, I tell Ashton what I have learned about the mysterious white car that went through the driveway and how I am almost positive that the car belonged to Caton's wife.

When he learns that I went over to the home of Caton's wife, he cautions me to be very careful and gives me a lecture. "Dana, there is a murderer running lose in this town and it may very well be someone in the school or someone who is associated with the school. I want you to be very careful. I can't lose you."

Ashton pauses as if waiting for my response, but I keep quiet. I know better than to try to argue with Ashton when he is upset.

He continues, "While it's okay for you and Reba to be sleuthing around a little, you have to be cautious. If the murderer suspects you are getting close to him or her, the person could go after you. If someone murders once, they sure can murder again. The thought of you being in danger scares the hell out of me."

I change the subject. "I'm so worried about going back to school on Monday. I only hope that Maybelle doesn't come to work. Wanda has a hearing in front of the school board on Tuesday night. I'm sure Maybelle's husband will support Wanda, and she may be back to work."

"I don't think Wanda will be back at work soon, Dana. She's being charged with battery of a child, and I can't imagine she'll be back in class for awhile."

"Don't count on it, Ashton. Wanda and Maybelle are both connivers who get away with more than they should."

Ashton shares, "I heard that Jason Estes's mother is a great attorney, and she is suing Mr. Estes for divorce. She not only pressed charges against Wanda, but is also calling for her immediate resignation from the district. Otherwise she plans to leave Estes penniless."

"I wish Wanda would resign. What a piece of work she is."

Ashton continues, "Wanda's husband has also filed for divorce so looks like Wanda may end up penniless and jobless. I sure don't feel sorry for anyone who hits a child. I hope Wanda gets what she deserves."

"Same here," I answer.

Then I proceed to tell Ashton what I have heard about Maybelle Clyde and her husband living way beyond their income.

Ashton reflects on his feelings about the Clydes, "Well we're going to be questioning Maybelle if she ate some of the pie. You know my gut has always said she and that high-fallutin husband of hers aren't what they're cracked up to be."

"Ashton, the omelet is ready. Let me refill your wine glass." I slide the omelet on a serving plate and refresh our wine.

As we sit down to enjoy our very late dinner, I ask Ashton about Mr. Bates, our custodian, and his nephew Elliott who is accused of raping Denise Flanigan.

"Elliott has admitted he was having sex with Denise, and is being held in the jail. He isn't able to post enough bond to get out. Your custodian doesn't seem to be involved even though Caton was blackmailing his nephew, Ellliott.

I ask, "Blackmailing Elliott, what do you mean?"

"Seems that Elliott was paying Caton $500 a month to keep his mouth shut. Caton knew he was messing around with Denise. I got to tell you, Dana, you've got a lot of slimy people in the school system."

"Tell me, I'm embarrassed by all of them. They don't give a good name to education."

"Glad there are a least a few of you who are working to help kids. Dana, this omelet is terrific. I think it's the best one I've ever had."

"Probably because you really worked up an appetite."

Ashton is always complimentary of my cooking.

I ask Ashton, "Do you want dessert? I've got ice cream, frozen yogurt, and cookies."

Ashton stands up and clears the table.
"Would love some dessert. How about you?"

As Ashton slips my robe off, we both forget about our problems.

CHAPTER 19

We are back in the real world of the classroom today after a busy Thanksgiving. Reba is in my classroom to visit this morning before the kids arrive. Reba can't believe what I told her that Maybelle said when she was questioned by the police about the cherry pie. "Maybelle has to be lying. She and Maddie had a piece of the pie at the same time. How could she say the pie tasted funny when Maddie said it tasted good to her?"

I answer, "She's clearly trying to say that Jenny put the fish oil in the pie when she made it."

Reba comments, "Maybelle has been out to get Jenny from the beginning. The only person Maybelle has any loyalty to is Wanda and herself."

"Turns out also that Andrea Depper, our secretary, said the pie was good when she ate it," I add.

Reba fishes for information, "Hey you look absolutely wonderful this morning, considering we are back at school today. You must have had quite a date with Ashton."

"It was a fantastic date and that's all I'm saying. Wish I could have a date like that every night."

I think back to our Saturday date, which finally ended at about six last night when Ashton had to go into work. We had spent most of the time in the bedroom, taking short breaks for meals. We never left the condo. Thinking back on the weekend makes me wonder whether marriage would be a good idea, but I'm still so scared to make that long-range commitment. I'm not alone. Ashton also has those fears. Could we make a marriage work or would it ruin the wonderful relationship we have? Waking up with Ashton is such a joy.

Reba interrupts my daydreaming, "You must be having some interesting thoughts right now from that smile on your face. Earth to Dana. Did Ashton say he's suspicious of Maybelle's story?"

"Ashton couldn't say much other than what I've told you, but I think he has Maybelle's number. Forgot to tell you, they're going to talk with Caton's wife today, and are hoping she can shed some light on who had motives to kill him."

Reba smirks, "Like everybody. Gotta go, I have some last minute copying I need to do before the kids get here. Let's have lunch in your classroom. I'll stop by Maddie's room and Sara's to ask them to join us. Glad Sara is going to be with us until Wanda gets back." Reba heads for the door.

"We can only hope that Wanda doesn't come back, but I guess we'll know after tomorrow night's hearing. I'm going to try to get my lessons back on target after the chaotic times we've had."

Thinking ahead to the week, I am looking forward to seeing my kids. I had a great social skills lesson I wanted to do on being thankful and never got to it before Thanksgiving because of all the craziness.

I can't wait to do my math lessons this week on my smartboard. The kids are really responding well to the clickers for their answers. I can put a problem on the board and give them possible answers and they have to click on what answer they believe is correct. They get to see the results of everyone's answers but don't know which classmates got the answer right and which students didn't.

I get the dialogue journals out and put them on each of the student's desk. Not having bus duty this morning, I have a little more prep time. Good thing because it will be a longer day than usual. I'm also on the planning committee for the holiday program, which we have to finalize after school.

"Good morning, Beth, how was your Thanksgiving vacation?" I greet one of my students who always comes in early, because her mom has to drop her off before she goes to work. She is eager to tell me about her trip to her grandma's and loves to help me pass out papers.

After Beth finishes her tale, and I put some stress balls on the students' desks, Beth looks up at me and says, "My mother thinks Mrs. Terrill should be fired for hitting Jason Estes. Do you think she should?"

Oh my, I'm thinking, how do I answer this one? I take a deep breath and say, "Beth, we have a school board that will decide that tomorrow evening." Just then the bell rings. I was literally saved by the bell.

The Thanksgiving vacation break has helped the students to forget some of the tragic events from the previous weeks, and we actually have a great morning.

I send the kids on to lunch and remind them before they go of the rules for the cafeteria. I give them a vote of confidence that I know they will behave well just like they have behaved this morning.

I go to the small frig that I have in my room. I take my chicken wrap and bottle of flavored water out, sit down at my small round table, take a breath, and go back to thoughts of my weekend with Ashton.

Maddie walks in. Shortly behind her are Sara and Reba.

Maddie says, "How was your morning? Mine was quiet."

Sara looks pretty tired and answers, "My morning was tough. I sure love subbing but being in Wanda's room is a challenge, especially with Jason in there. He is so angry about what Wanda did to him, and I can't say that I blame him."

Reba says, "Isn't it interesting that a few teachers are back in the teacher's lounge now. It's no longer closed off, but I sure don't want to eat in there after what happened. I'm not sure I'll ever eat another piece of cherry pie again."

Maddie speculates, "Hey, Mr. Bates is not back to work, and I see that we have another substitute janitor. How many does that make now? Three. I thought sure he would be back. He hasn't been charged with anything."

Reba projects, "What to do about his status is on the board agenda for tomorrow night. That should be some board meeting. Looks like it will last til 2 in the morning."

Sara comments, "I heard there's going to be a big crowd."

I am reminded of what I saw and how I have to convey it to the Board in executive session. I say, "Don't remind me about it. I have to be there because I was a witness, and they are going to decide what to do with Wanda. I sure want to skip it."

Reba tells about her trip to the office this morning, "Not to change the subject but I had an interesting conversation with Andrea Depper while I was copying a short study guide for my kiddos. Seems she's trying to reconcile the student activity fund. She knows that some of the events made more money than the financial statements show. Our acting principal told her he needs a report for the superintendent, and she is having a lot of trouble doing it."

I say, "Funny you would say that because she commented on that fund the day Caton called me into the office. Wonder what's going on?"

Reba continues, "What was most interesting is this. She asked me whether something was going on with Maybelle and Caton and the activity fund. Seems she overheard them one day arguing in his office about how much money the chili supper made. When they realized that she might be able to hear them, Caton quickly closed the door."

Sara is curious, "The student activity fund? The chili supper? What's going on?"

Reba adds, "Their voices then got very quiet, and when Maybelle came out of his office, she was smiling like a Cheshire cat and seemed pleased with herself."

CHAPTER 20

There must be more than 200 people in this school board meeting. Some of the teachers from school are here and quite a few community members who are curious as to what the board is going to do about everything that has happened in the schools.

The boardroom connects to the palatial Superintendent's office in a room that has a large U shaped walnut table with microphones on it and speaker phones. The superintendent's office is the size of my classroom with beautiful paintings, high back chairs, and a couch. An oriental rug covers the hardwood floors. Within the boardroom, there is a separate sitting area for the press and there are at least ten reporters here. I bet they are not only from our community but from some of those around us. After all, how often is a school principal murdered at a school? How often does a teacher rape a student? How often does a teacher hit a student? How many people would believe this could happen in what was always a nice quiet community.

While there are 50 seats for audience members, there sure aren't enough for tonight's crowd. Reba and I got here early for the meeting because we figured it would be crowded, and I am nervous enough without having to stand up the whole time.

Reba says, "Can you believe this crowd. I'm glad we got here early."

I answer, "I guess everyone wants some excitement, and they sure have it now in our schools."

Memories go back to the day when I got called in to Caton's office for reporting my observation that Wanda hit Jason Estes. Now I sit in the school board meeting waiting for the executive session where I will be questioned by the entire board, including Maybelle's husband, about what I saw. Mr. Bates, our custodian, is in the back row since his job is on the firing line. He will also be asked about what he saw the day Caton suspended him.

The usual minutes and bills are approved, and the state of two of the schools is discussed. The board would love to close two buildings, even though they are high achieving schools. I can't imagine they will ever pass a referendum to construct new schools with this economy, and now with all this negative publicity.

With all their open business out of the way, Maybelle's husband makes a motion to go into executive session for purposes of discussing personnel, and the motion is seconded and approved. Executive session begins at around 7:30.

The board president announces, "We are now moving into executive session and I ask all of our audience members to wait outside, and we will call you back in at the appropriate time."

Needless to say there aren't enough chairs so most of us pull our chairs from the board meeting. Some just go to the hall and take a seat on the floor, knowing it's going to be a long night.

The superintendent comes over to me and reminds me that I am expected to stay until I am called. He goes over and tells Mr. Bates the same and when I look around I see Jason Estes' mother and Jason. The superintendent talks to them. I'm sure he's conveying the same message to all of us.

After two hours of standing or sitting in the hall, Mrs. Estes and Jason are called in.

Reba looks over at me, "I wonder how long they will be in there."

"Who knows, I'm so worried about how long I will be questioned, I haven't thought about them."

We wait and wait, and at least another hour goes by and Mrs. Estes and Jason come out. The superintendent follows and looks at me, "Dana, we're ready for you now."

Reba whispers to me, "You'll do fine, Dana."

By now it is about 11:00. I follow the superintendent in and he closes the door. Here I go to face the firing line. I take the chair that is set up for witnesses who are testifying. I am facing all the board members. The chairman of the board, Alfonse Nollwood asks me, "Will you tell the board members exactly what you witnessed."

I explain precisely what I saw and how Wanda had hit a student.

Maybelle's husband asks, "Are you sure you saw her hit the student?"

I answer, "Yes, I did."

He then asks, "How do you know that the student was indeed Jason Estes?"

I explain that since I was involved in extracurricular activities in which Jason had participated, I knew him. No other board members asked any questions.

When I come out after about only twenty minutes, I wonder how I did. I thought I was well prepared and answered board member questions.

Mrs. Estes comes over to me, "I just want to thank you for being a witness to what happened to my son. The Department of Children and Family Services told me that you filed a report. I'm so grateful that there are good teachers like you who take your job seriously. Whatever happens, I won't forget what you did to protect Jason."

I am taken aback because I had taken so much guff from Caton about my report. It was nice to hear someone appreciate what I had done. I answer, "Thank you, Mrs. Estes, I am a required reporter, and I'm so sorry this happened to Jason. I hope everything turns out okay."

I have to wonder anymore what is okay. It won't be okay if Wanda is back in the classroom, but she may be.

Reba asks me, "Dana, are you alright?"

"I'm fine." I have to be cautious of what I say because there are so many people standing around. I know I'm not supposed to share what happened in executive session.

I look over to see Mr. Bates who smiles at me. I smile back a vote of confidence that I know he is innocent, and I hope he gets his job back. He looks like he's aged 20 years after what we have been through with our observation of Wanda, and what has happened to the nephew he loved and believed had such a promising educational career ahead of him.

The board secretary comes out and asks for Mr. Bates to come in. I tell him good luck. I know that he may not have a job after tonight because he isn't protected by the union.

I whisper to Reba, "Seems so unfair that Mr. Bates may be punished for doing his job and reporting Wanda, but also because he's related to Elliott."

"Caton still does his damage from the grave. and I bet Wanda will get off tonight," Reba whispers to me.

"The night is young," I whisper back.

The board finally comes out of executive session and takes action publicly with almost all 200 observers still there. The board votes to remove Wanda Terrill from her position and to recommend to the State Teacher Licensure Board that her teaching license be revoked. There is one dissenting vote. Maybelle's husband votes against the motion.

    I comment as Reba and I walk to the car around 2 a.m. "I just can't believe it. Sometimes justice does prevail."

    Reba answers, "I've never seen Wanda look so beaten down, and Maybelle wouldn't even look at us. Can you believe Maybelle's husband voted in favor of keeping Wanda?"

    I say, "That figures since Maybelle and Wanda are such good buds."

    Reba responds, "Luckily the other school board members have some brains. I'm so delighted that they are recommending that the State Teacher Licensure Board revoke her teaching license. They really gave her a double whammy with firing her and doing that. It will be difficult for her to ever get another job, at least in this state. What a stand for our usually wimpy school board members. How did you do when you went into Executive Session?"

    Reba is still trying to figure out what happened in private.

    I answer very carefully, "I had my notes with me, and I just reiterated what I saw. I was more composed than I thought I would ever be. Not to change the subject, but you know the big thing to me is that the board voted to have Mr. Bates come back to work, and award him back pay for the days that Caton suspended him. I'm surprised they did that because of his nephew."

    Reba offers her opinion, "Bates' nephew will probably serve time in prison. I'm not surprised that Elliott was fired and will also be recommended to lose his teaching certificate. What a fool he was! Course, unfortunately other teachers do that kind of garbage and don't get caught. Hopefully this will scare some teachers into thinking twice before they mess around with students."

"Reba, so true, you know we've been so tied up in this mess with Wanda that we have to get back to figuring out who killed Caton. We know it wasn't Jenny, but she's in a heap of trouble if we can't help figure out who really did it."

Reba answers, "Tomorrow night is the memorial service for Caton. Let's keep our ears open there. Wish we could get some more time alone with his wife. She's got to know more about what's going on. I still want to know why she was driving through the parking lot."

CHAPTER 21

"That was a strange memorial service, wasn't it?" Reba whispers to me as we leave the very abbreviated form of a ceremony to honor the life of someone. "There weren't hardly any flowers."

I am talking in a low tone of voice, afraid that someone is listening to me, "I can't believe that only Caton's brother gave a tribute besides the minister. Lots of people knew Caton so why didn't anyone else make comments?"

"Because everyone hated him," Reba answers.

"I think the minister thought more people would comment. Did you see the way Caton's wife looked around to see whether other people were going to come forward to speak about him? That poor woman."

Reba asks, "Should we go downstairs a few minutes to get some refreshments? I know the church ladies here usually put on a big spread after funerals." Reba is always thinking about food, that's why I am surprised she didn't have any of the infamous cherry pie the day Caton was murdered.

I agree, "Definitely, let's go downstairs. I could use a hot cup of decaf, and we need to snoop around, and see what else we can find out. Poor Jenny is in big trouble if we don't find the murderer. I hope they don't have any pie tonight."

The smell of freshly brewed coffee, meatballs, and barbecue sauce makes the basement more inviting. There are a number of people I have never seen before. They must be relatives of Caton and his wife.

In the corner, I see Caton's mother and father who seem to be in a state of shock. My mother always said there is nothing worse than losing a child of your own. My heart goes out to these people. I decide to approach them and Reba follows me.

"Mr. and Mrs. Caton, my name is Dana Lawrence, and this is Reba Krell. We want to express our deepest sympathy to you. We're teachers in the building where your son was principal. Do you live here in town?"

Caton's mother seems to be a nice lady but is very small and frail, probably in her 70s. She smiles and comments, "Thank you for coming. We're happy to meet some of the people our son worked with. We live in Louisville." She sighs as she continues, "We always wished that our son would have stayed closer to home to work but he was eager to move away and we didn't get to see him much. Typical boy, we hardly heard from him unless we called to see how he was doing."

Reba answers, "You're right. That's a man for you."

Caton's mother continues, "Lauren was always good to have our grandson and granddaughter call us. You know they are the only grandchildren we have. We hope Lauren will consider moving back."

I ask, "How did your son and Lauren meet?"

"She and Jimmie met at the University of Louisville, and we thought sure they would stay. But Jimmie had other ideas. He wanted to move away and convinced Lauren there was a whole new world out there. Between us, I don't think Lauren has ever liked living here in Hallicott City. You know it just doesn't have the opportunities that we have in Louisville."

Caton's father is afraid that Grace has insulted us but under the circumstances, we know that people say unusual things when they are in mourning, "Now, Grace, not everyone wants to live in Louisville and these two nice young ladies may have been raised here, and think it's wonderful. Anyway, we're so glad you came here tonight. It means a lot to us."

Caton's brother approaches us. Grace comments, "Oh, Will, these nice ladies teach in the building where Jimmy was the principal. Dana and Reba, right?"

I answer, "Yes, you certainly have a good memory. Good to meet you Will. Do you live in Louisville also?"

"I'm not far away. I live in Lexington. I'm a CPA and primarily do work for clients who have horses. I also have some clients in Louisville so get there often. I'm just the opposite of Jimmie. I like to stay close to home. Jimmie was my big brother. He's 9 years older than me. I feel so bad that we didn't spend more time together."

"We're so sorry about your brother and please know you have our sympathy," Reba comments.

I add, "We hope they figure out soon who did this to your brother."

Grace speaks up, "How could anyone do that to my son? I only hope he didn't suffer too long. The police said they are doing their best to find the murderer, and we hope when they do, they send the person to the electric chair."

Caton's father replies, "Grace, the police will see that the person is brought to justice in whatever way is possible. We are going to stay here until they finish their work. We hope Lauren will move back home with the kids so we can provide her with support, and get to know them all well. Jimmie was always so protective of them that he never let us get too close. That was Jimmie for you. Always possessive with what was his."

I say, "If there is anything we can do for you, just let us know. If you'll excuse us, we'll let you talk to some other people." We move away to the coffee.

Reba grabs each of us a plate, and starts to fill hers. "Oh, this looks good. I didn't have any supper."

There are small meatballs in chili sauce, a cheese and relish tray, brownies, a white sheet cake, and sugar cookies.

Just as I've filled my plate, I hear Maybelle's voice. "I can't believe the two of you have the nerve to show up for Caton's funeral after all the trouble you've caused."

Maybelle's husband, who is on the school board and who voted to keep Wanda in her job, speaks up, "Now, Maybelle, be nice. After all these two do teach in the building and worked with Caton, although Dana caused him so much grief after what she did to poor Wanda."

I have to defend myself, "Excuse me, Mr. Clyde, but I was just doing my job in reporting what I saw, and I don't think this conversation is appropriate at a funeral."

Maybelle smirks at me as she speaks with her common sarcastic tone, "You certainly are defensive. Makes me wonder what you have to hide, Dana. Do you take fish oil?"

Reba pulls me away as I am seething mad. "Let's go. We want to express our condolences to Mrs. Caton, and we don't have to stand here and respond to such a question. Maybe you ought to be discussing your finances, rather than asking us questions."

"Maybelle's husband is as bad as she is. Good for you, Reba, that was a good dig at both of them. We may both be looking for a new job next school year. Let's go over to Lauren and then get out of here. Have you noticed there are only two other teachers from our building here? Guess that says what the people in our building thought of Caton."

We approach Caton's wife, Lauren. Reba says, "Mrs. Caton, we want to tell you how sorry we are about your loss. If there is anything we can do to help you, please let us know."

I nod in agreement with what Reba is saying.

"It was kind of you to stop by the house the other night. I'm glad you told me to check my tire. It was a bit low on air. That car has caused me lots of problems. I think I'll probably get rid of it."

I ask, "What are your plans, if you don't mind us asking. We talked to your husband's parents, and they are hoping you will move back to Louisville, so they can see your beautiful children more. Is your family from there also?"

"Yes, my parents actually live in Elizabethtown, which is right outside Louisville and now that James is gone, I will probably need to go back to work and would like to return to teaching. James never wanted me to work as a teacher since he was a principal, but now I don't have much choice. If you know anybody who wants to buy a house, let me know."

Reba replies, "We'll keep our ears open."

Lauren does sound serious about leaving eventually. She continues, "I'm determined to stay here til they find out who did such a horrible thing to James. It's interesting isn't it? You always think that a school is safe but in so many ways, it isn't. This whole town certainly changed our life for the worst. Tomorrow I have to speak to the police and see how I can help them solve my husband's murder."

I add, "If you'll excuse us, we need to get going. Please take care of yourself and your children. We wish you the best."

As we walk away pondering the interesting responses we got from Lauren Caton, I comment to Reba, "You and I have a lot to digest from this evening, and not just the food. Let's get out of here."

Reba stops me as she sees our school secretary, "Wait a minute. There's Andrea and her husband. Let's go over and talk to them first."

I extend my sympathy to Andrea, "Hi, Andrea, I know this must be very hard on you losing Caton. After all you were his secretary this year."

Andrea's husband, Carl, comments, "This really has been tough for her. She worked so hard for Caton, even though he didn't appreciate her very much."

"Oh, Carl, I'm not sure Caton really knew how to appreciate anyone," Andrea responds.

Carl keeps talking, "And then, the police questioned her after school to see if she could shed any light on what happened to Caton. They asked her how that cherry pie tasted when she ate a piece."

Andrea adds, "I did have an interesting conversation with the police and told them the pie tasted fine when I had it. I know that Jenny would never put anything bad in a pie. I told them they better question Maybelle since she had a piece of it."

Andrea then changes the subject: "I thought more teachers from school would be here at the funeral. It's sad how so many of them didn't like him."

"I'm surprised that Maybelle is here," Reba comments.

Andrea adds, "Oh, that certainly doesn't surprise me. They were real, real close, if you know what I mean. I 'm surprised that the two of you didn't know that."

CHAPTER 22

Many teachers live for Friday afternoons. This Friday was cause for celebration here at Lincoln School since another difficult week was over. There were still no arrests but lots of questioning of more suspects in Caton's murder.

I was breathing a sigh of relief that I had gotten through the school board meeting, the preparations for the holiday program, and the memorial service for Caton. I had kept my students calm amidst the holiday season, and the excitement of some light snowfall this afternoon.

The kids were now gone and I was just sitting at my desk.

Reba comes in my door looking as tired as I feel. "Hey, Dana, bring out the diet cokes. I brought some microwave popcorn. Let's celebrate."

"Sounds good to me," I answer.

"Can you believe we made it through the week. I stopped by Maddie and Sara's room and told them to join us for some down time."

"Hi guys, did I hear a party's going on in here?" Enter Maddie with Sara right behind her. I notice that Sara's hair is more frizzy than usual and her reading glasses are sliding down her face. Maddie, on the other hand, looks like she just walked out of a salon without a strand of hair out of place.

"Have a drink," I say as I serve my buddies their cans of soda and Reba empties the popcorn onto four napkins. "A diet caffeine free coke is as good as I can do."

Maddie is curious about how things are going for Sara, and asks, "Sara, are things better in your room now that the students know Wanda isn't coming back? Is Jason settled down?"

The school intercom begins its buzz. We all get quiet anticipating what message is coming from the other end.

"Sara, will you please report to the office immediately?"

Sara says, "Uh, oh, what have I done? Save my coke for me til I get back. I better get down there."

Sara gets up, scoots her chair in, and heads to the door.

"Good luck, Sara, if they're arresting you we'll post bond." Reba jokes, then adds. "I'm just kidding, Sara, good luck. We'll wait for you."

Reba turns her attention to Maddie, and says, "So tell us about what the police asked you?" Maddie had been questioned by the police and we wonder what happened.

"Well they didn't say much. They asked me if I ate a piece of the cherry pie, when I ate it, and how it tasted. I told them that the pie tasted good, and I ate a piece about twelve fifteen. I remember the time because I had my lunch in the lounge and grabbed a piece for dessert. I love Jenny's pies and cakes.

Reba comments, "You sure were precise."

Maddie continues, "I told them that I had one of Jenny's pies before and it was as good as ever. After I ate the pie, that was the last time I went to the lounge that day. I still can't believe somebody killed Caton with fish oil. Who do you guys think did it?"

I answer, "There are lots of people who had a motive. I've made a list of them. Elliott could have done it, Wanda may have. Maybelle could have. Mrs. Caton could have. After all we know she was driving through the parking lot that night."

Reba adds, "The police haven't ruled out Jenny but we know she wouldn't murder anyone. They probably haven't ruled out Mr. Bates."

I interject, "They haven't ruled me out either but Ashton knows I couldn't do such a thing."

Reba asks, "Speaking of Ashton, what is on the agenda for this weekend. Ashton must be going nuts with this investigation. Is he going to have time for any big dates with you? Maybe there's going to be a ring under the Christmas tree."

I answer, "Oh, Reba, ever the eternal optimist. Don't count on a ring. We're not ready for that. Ashton is hoping to come over later tonight. I'm fixing my chicken divan recipe. Tomorrow night we are scheduled to go to the Symphony's Christmas program. Speaking of Christmas programs, I have to get some more practices in for my kids for our school's program. That's coming up in a few days."

Maddie responds, "Can you believe we only have one more week until Christmas break. I'm going nuts trying to get everything done."

I voice my frustration, "Well I'm determined to figure out before our break who murdered Caton. This is horrible the way this is hanging over us."

Maddie questions, "Has anybody heard what happened with Maybelle? Was she questioned by the police yesterday?"

Reba replies, "Don't mention that woman's name to me. Andrea almost came out and said that Maybelle was having an affair with Caton. Have you heard anything about that, Maddie?"

Maddie answers, "I can't believe I was so stupid I haven't seen what was going on. And Maybelle has the nerve to criticize us! "Every time I think about Maybelle, I get angry."

Sara walks back in my room looking like she is ready to explode with anger. Her face is flushed and her voice is as loud as I have ever heard it. "Did I hear Maybelle's name being blasted? Let me join the crowd."

I question Sara, "What happened. Why were you called to the office?"

Sara blurts this shocking statement, "Now I'm a suspect in Caton's murder."

We all open our mouths, and Reba speaks first, "Wait a minute. You have to be kidding. That's absurd."

Sara explains, "This morning, Maybelle met with Mr. Thomas and told him that I was talking about Wanda during classes. She said I told the class that Wanda was a bad teacher and deserved to be kicked out."

I say," Maybelle did what?"

Sara continues, "I told Thomas that I had done no such thing, and I have been very careful not to discuss the previous teacher. It made me so mad that I went on to tell him that Wanda had never left any lesson plans for me. I have created all of my own based on the common core standards. I also told him the kids said they did worksheets all day with Wanda."

"Wait a minute how does that make you a suspect in Caton's murder?" I am confused by what Sara is saying and need more information.

"It's horrible and I'm so shocked that Mr. Thomas would even believe this about me. Maybelle told him that I hated Caton because my husband, Derek, was involved in a case against Caton, and my husband lost the case. Maybelle claims she heard me say to the students that Caton got what he deserved."

I say, "Oh Sara, I'm so sorry you have to deal with the wrath of Maybelle. She's a snake."

Sara is now in tears as she says, "Now I'm going to be questioned by the police, and Thomas will be talking to the superintendent to see if I can work in the district anymore. Can you believe that woman can lie and get away with it?"

CHAPTER 23

My phone call to Mother on the way home from school to what I hoped was a relaxing weekend with Ashton yields a surprise. "You heard what, Mother?" What do you mean?"

On the other end I hear, "I tell you Dana, my bridge buddies heard that Maybelle was having an affair with Caton. Caton's wife knew it and she was planning to file for divorce. Guess she never got to do it before he was murdered. Everybody thinks she probably did it."

"My goodness, Mother, your friends sure hear a lot of news."

Mother continues, "I told them you saw her car drive through the parking lot the night it happened. Think about it, Dana, she certainly would know her husband was allergic to fish oil."

"But Mother, I just saw her drive through the lot. I didn't see her stop."

"I know that but she could have easily come back. I feel sure it had to be her."

"Mother, I just don't think it's that easy. My money is on Maybelle. Maybe he jilted her, and she wanted to get even."

"Well I'm betting I'm right. See what you can find out tonight. Isn't Ashton coming over to dinner at your place?"

"He sure is. I've got my chicken divan casserole ready and in the frig. Catch you later Mother."

Ashton comes over and we are finishing our meal.

"Wow that chicken divan was wonderful and I sure like the candlelight and wine. You really know how to get to my heart." Ashton is leaning back in his chair looking very satisfied.

"I have dessert too."

"Oh, I know, I can't wait." Ashton has this look of anticipation on his face for a long night together.

"No, I'm talking about a pre-dessert before you and me have our real dessert. I made a cherry chocolate dump cake."

"Next to you, you know that's my favorite."

We're just finishing up the dump cake. I relay my conversation with my Mother about the latest on Maybelle and Caton having an affair, and Caton's wife finding out about it.

"I can't imagine that she would kill the father of her children. I know you saw her driving through the parking lot, but I bet she was just checking out whether he was really working late at school. She had to be tired of the long hours he was keeping.

"That's kind of what I thought, but wanted to tell you what Mother heard."

Ashton comments, "I'm going to check that story out. We need all the leads we can get even if some of them are unsubstantiated rumors. Okay, enough business I'm going to clean up so we can get to more important things."

"Better idea. I'll help and we can move on even faster. I have really missed you. Let's hope there are no phone calls tonight."

The table is cleared, and the dishwasher loaded in record time. Ashton switches the lights off, and leads me to the bedroom.

I awaken to that heavenly smell of coffee and bacon frying. I slip on my robe and make a quick trip to the bathroom; I head to the kitchen to see the glorious sight of Ashton in his t-shirt and jeans cooking breakfast. I could get used to this.

Ashton plants a kiss on my lips, and says, "Hey sleepyhead, good morning. What a night! I hope we can do the same tonight."

I suggest, "Sounds like a plan to me. Then again I have a better idea. We can do it all day and all night."

"I like that even better, and in that case it's a good thing I'm making a big breakfast. Wait a minute, we have one errand we need to do. I thought we were going to the new boutique so you could help me pick up a gift for my mom and sister."

Ashton's mother lives here in town and his sister, a nurse, lives about four hours away. I really like both of them. We'll spend Christmas eve with them, then Ashton and I will spend Christmas day with my family.

"Oops, you're right. Well they don't open until 10 so we've got a couple of hours to do what we want. Any ideas?"

Our trip to the boutique is fun because we are able to get a great sweater set for his Mother and a cape for his sister. Both are perfect gifts for each of them. I love this new boutique that Jenny's cousin operates. I was hoping we would get to see Jenny, but she isn't scheduled to come in to help until this afternoon.

As we head back to my place in Ashton's car, his phone rings. Ashton answers and listens and then comments, "Give me 15 minutes to get there"

"I guess that means our plans are on hold for awhile?" I ask.

Ashton answers, "This shouldn't take too long, Dana. Believe me I'll try to get back as soon as I can. I have been picturing you and me in front of your fireplace after I saw some of that lingerie at the boutique. I'll drop you off and get back as quick as I can."

After Ashton drops me off, I decide to use the time to clean up the apartment and get a few gifts wrapped and put under the tree. I've just finished making some cheese dip, and chilling the wine, when my cell rings.

Ashton comments over the phone. "Be there in five minutes. I'm thinking about the fireplace and what you're wearing and I'm on my way back. Do you think we can skip the symphony tonight? I just want to spend the time with you."

I answer the door with my sheerest lingerie on and a glass of wine in my hand.

"Wow, you look incredible and what a greeting."

Much later after our time together in front of the fireplace I ask Ashton whether he was able to get some work done. Ashton tells me that they have questioned Mrs. Caton more this afternoon looking for any lead they can get.

Ashton looks puzzled as he says, "Something now is really bothering me about Mrs. Caton. I feel sorry for her, and can't imagine she would kill her husband, but when we got to her house we were surprised to see her surrounded by boxes. When we asked her if she was moving after the case was solved, she told us that she planned to get out of town as fast as she could. She didn't care when the case was solved, she was moving anyway."

CHAPTER 24

Our holiday program is over. The kids and audience have all gone home. Only Reba and I are left in the auditorium.

I comment, "At last, this holiday program is over. This was just one more piece of stress I didn't need."

Reba reminds me of our holiday break. "Considering everything that has been on the kids' minds not to mention ours, it sure went well. Now only 3 more days, and it is 2 weeks of rest and relaxation."

I sigh, "I wish we could solve this murder before break. I just keep thinking that there has to be an important piece of information we are missing but I can't figure it out."

With all the craziness here at our school, very few people wanted to help with the holiday program, so the brunt of the work had fallen on Reba and me. The school system is too cheap to pay Mr. Bates, our custodian, to work at night so we get the honor of janitorial duties.

I say, "Well let's get this place picked up quick and get out of here. This whole school is so spooky now since it's a murder scene, and I've always thought this auditorium is creepy anyway. It's so dark and depressing."

Reba adds, "I don't like this place any more than you. The quicker we get out of here the better."

I provide a plan. "You take the front part of the room and I'll take the back and we'll meet in the middle and have this placed cleaned up in no time. We didn't even serve food but look at the candy wrappers and all the garbage I've already got. The place smells like barbecue and cigarettes combined. Did somebody actually bring a pizza in here?"

Reba answers, "I think there must have been pizza, because I smell it too."

I say in a loud voice, "Gee I wish Mr. Bates was here tonight to do this. When I have to pick up after other people I really appreciate him, that's for sure."

"Somebody even threw a cigarette butt on the floor." Reba yells back at me. "Cigarettes are illegal in schools. Some people will try anything."

No more than Reba gets the sentence out of her mouth, the already dim and dreary room goes dark. I panic. I can't see anything. "Hey Reba, did you hit the light switch up there?"

The place is pitch black. I hate the dark and know Reba does too. We've often talked about how we are afraid of the dark. It reminds us of falling into a black hole. I can't get my bearings. Where am I?

"I thought you did, Dana, the light switches are back where you are. Dana, I'm scared. I can't see anything."

I hear footsteps and say, "Reba is that you?"

A deep voice comes out of the darkness. "You nosy bitch. Quit tellin that boyfriend of yours what's going on."

I try to open my mouth to speak. As I do, I feel a stabbing pain in my arm. I hear myself let out a groan, and I sink to the floor.

Reba yells, "Dana, was that you? What's up? Where are you?"

All I can do is let out a low moaning sound.

"Dana, did you fall? I'm trying to find you. Hang on. I've got my cell in my pocket, thank goodness. I can't find the lights. I'm calling nine one one."

The last thing I hear is Reba's voice. "Help, we're at Lincoln School in the auditorium."

I hear voices and am struggling to wake up. I'm on the floor. The lights are back on. I see blood covering my arm.

Reba is saying, "We were just here cleaning up when the lights went out."

I wince from the pain but smile when I hear Ashton's voice. "Can you hear me, Dana, the ambulance is here. The paramedics are going to move you on to the stretcher. Just relax."

I whisper, "I wish I could relax. My arm hurts. What's all this blood? Was I stabbed? Who turned the lights off?"

Ashton says in a low voice, "It's going to be okay. We'll figure out what happened." I've called your mother and she's going to meet us at the hospital."

I raise my voice as much as I can. "Oh my god, am I dying? Why did you call my mother?" I start crying.

Ashton says, "Take it easy, Dana, someone hurt you. You're going to be okay. We just need to get you to the hospital. Reba's going to ride in the ambulance with you. I'll meet you there. Somebody hurt your arm and we probably need to get some stitches for you."

I guess it must be the paramedics raising my body onto the stretcher into the ambulance. My arm hurts so bad. Get me to the hospital quick and stop this sharp pain.

Reba's voice grabs my attention. "Dana, how are you doing? I am so sorry about all of this. We should have just left the place a mess. It won't take long to get to St. John's."

I feel like I'm rambling but can't seem to keep quiet. "Reba, it's not your fault. My arm really hurts. I just remember a sharp pain and then something warm gushing out. It must have been my blood. Are you okay? Did they get you? Did they say anything to you?"

Reba answers, "No, Dana, I'm fine. Just scared of what's happening."

I want to sleep but the pain's so bad. I think somebody has covered my arm with a bandage. The ambulance is slowing down and comes to a stop. The paramedics come around and my stretcher is being moved again.

"Brr, it's cold out here. Get me inside." I turn to Reba.

The intake nurse greets me, "That's a pretty bad gash you got. Tell me what happened. Were you in a fight?"

I'm feeling weak and light headed. I know I have to stay awake and tell what I remember before I go back to sleep.

My words stumble out, "Reba and I cleaning up after school show. She was in front of auditorium. Me in back. Lights went out. So black."

The nurse asks, "You were in the school auditorium when this happened?

I move my head up and down, "I just thought Reba hit switch and I yelled at her."

I look at Reba and say, "Sorry, Reba."

Reba is there beside me, "Don't worry about that, Dana, just tell what you remember."

I say, "Heard footsteps. Somebody by me who told me to mind business. Felt a sharp stabbing in my arm. Called me a nosy bitch and told me quit giving information to Ashton. Ashton, police officer, my boyfriend." I smile.

"I'm gonna find that son of a bitch," says Ashton who must be very angry, and having trouble controlling his temper. He lowers his voice and asks, "Was it a male or female voice? Did you recognize it?"

I tell what I remember, "Male. Don't think he was alone. Smelled like cigarette but perfume smell too. That's all I can think of."

"That's great," Ashton comments. "This is helpful to us. Maybe a man and a woman."

The emergency room doctor has come in the room and, after looking at me, comments, "We need to get you stitched up. This is a nasty gash and you've lost some blood. The good news is you're going to be just fine. You need to take it easy for the next day or so."

The doctor is interrupted in his instructions with the arrival of my mother and brother. My mother rushes over to me. "Oh Dana, are you okay?"

Mother then looks at the doctor: "Is my daughter going to be all right?"

"I'm Dr. Hogan. I was just telling Dana she's going to be okay but she needs to get some rest and take tomorrow off after the trauma she suffered tonight. She'll be able to go home after I get her stitched up, but she must be watched very closely for the next twenty-four hours."

My brother, Bud, adds, "Thanks, Doctor. Dana can either go to my Mom's and stay there or Mom can go back to Dana's condo with her. She could come to our house but it sure isn't very quiet and peaceful there. I'll check on her as much as I can."

I notice that Ashton is trying to signal my brother. "Bud, can I see you out in the hall a minute?"

CHAPTER 25

The ER doctor looks at me again. I have been poked and prodded enough times tonight. I'm worn out, and just want to get out of here and go to bed. Isn't it amazing how you can be in a private room in an ER and hear everything going on? I've heard people puking, kids crying, and people complaining of minor aches and pains for which I wouldn't even dream of going to an emergency room. The smell of vomit is the worst.

"Dana, I'm going to give you a shot that will relax you and deaden the pain so you can be stitched up in a little while. My assistant will come in and fix your arm up so we can get you out of here."

I question the doctor, "Is my arm gonna be all right?"

Dr. Hogan answers, "Your arm's going to be stiff and sore awhile but I think a couple of Tylenol every 4 hours will help. I'm going to refer you back to your doctor, Dr. Princhard, so you can do the follow up with him. You may have some scarring, but unless you're going to be an arm model, it won't be bad."

"I just have to be able to write. I'm a teacher."

"Don't worry about that. You'll be able to write."

The doctor then looks at my mother. "Mrs. Lawrence, since you're going to be watching Dana tomorrow, please let her doctor know right away if there is any unusual bleeding or if she becomes disoriented. She may be a little nauseated from the antibiotics I'm giving her."

Dr. Hogan and my mother go back out in the hall.

Reba comes back in the room. She looks so scared and worried.

I say, "Reba, you have to be exhausted." Reba is my dearest friend and my heart goes out to her. She's always there for me.

Reba says to me, "Dana, we've got to solve this murder, we can't let whoever did this get away with it. I don't want you to get hurt. Why don't you stay home for a couple of days and just come back on Friday for the party."

"Reba, I have so much to do to get ready for the kids' holiday party on Friday. I can stay home tomorrow but I have to be back on Thursday."

"Dana, you have to be shook about this mess. I sure am. I'm so worried and so glad you're going to be okay. Don't worry about tomorrow. I asked Ashton to call Mr. Thomas to get a sub for you tomorrow."

"Thanks, Reba, I sure don't feel like going back to school tomorrow."

Reba continues, "Thomas has been filled in on the latest happening at Lincoln. When will it ever end?"

Ashton and Bud show their faces back in my cubicle. I frown from a mixture of pain and apprehension. I hope that shot takes effect pretty soon.

At the same time, I'm so happy to see them. Their concern shows on their faces. "Okay guys, what's the big secret? You two went out in the hall to talk. I know something's up. Have you figured out who did this to me?"

Ashton answers, "Dana, you know that what happened to you is no accident. Someone wants you to stay out of the picture. We have to put you on police protection until we solve this."

I raise my voice, "Police protection? How are you going to do that?"

Ashton says, "I want you to go to your mother's, and stay there until we say you can go home. We're going to have a police car outside the house. I know you. You don't want to miss school on Thursday and Friday. We are going to have protection at school also.

Ashton looks at Reba. "Reba, we're going to have a police officer at the school tomorrow to make sure you're safe. You two have gotten too close to the murderer, and we can't take any chances."

The look on Ashton's face is one of fright and concern. Even though I've dated Ashton quite awhile, I have never seen such a worried look on his face. I feel so much warmth toward him while he's talking. It gives me great comfort to know that he is watching out for me.

Reba jumps up. "Ashton, we have to catch this horrible person. Who can it be? Do you think it's a husband and wife team or a lover and accomplice team? So many people had a motive. What male and female together wanted Caton dead?"

I answer, "At least I'll have a day off to think."

The shot has obviously taken effect because I'm feeling very tired and my arm isn't hurting as much as it was earlier.

The Physician's Assistant comes in. "Gee it looks like you have quite a fan club, Dana. Can I ask all of you to step out so I can get these stitches in, and then we can let you take Dana home."

I don't feel much of anything when I'm stitched up. I turn my head away because I don't want to see anything that's being done to my arm.

The PA finishes up and tells me he is giving me a prescription for an antibiotic, then I'll be free to go. My "fan club" returns.

It reassures me when Ashton says, "Dana, I'll take you to your Mother's. Reba, I'll take you back to school to get your car and follow you home. Glad you picked up Dana for the holiday program, so we don't have to worry about getting Dana's car home."

Bud announces, "I'll meet you at Mom's, Dana."

I answer, "Thanks Bud for bringing Mother, and for being here. Ashton, school is right on the way to Mother's so let's just drop Reba off first. I'll be fine. I'm just a little sleepy."

On the way to Mother's, we stop at school and as Reba gets ready to hop out of Ashton's car to get in hers, Ashton blurts out, "Wait a minute, Reba, I don't think you're going to be driving that car anywhere tonight."

I'm almost asleep but my ears perk up. "What's the matter, I thought we were going to follow Reba home in her car?"

"Oh no." Reba blurts out, "My car. It's ruined."

Even though it's dark, we can see that the tires are flat, and the front windshield and back window are smashed to bits.

CHAPTER 26

I have settled in at mothers. Ashton dropped me off late last night. I tossed all night with my mind trying to figure out who attacked me and who messed up Reba's car.

My cell phone rings. It's good to hear Ashton's voice on the other end. "Dana, I want to come over in a little while. Are you feeling up to it?"

"Definitely come over. Mother isn't letting me do anything. I'm about to go nuts."

Ashton says, "I'm glad she's taking care of you."

"Reba called over lunch. She said there was a new sub in my room, and she has never been at the school before. They couldn't get anybody they've had, since it's too close to the holidays. Probably everyone is afraid to come to our jinxed school."

"I can understand that," Ashton responds.

I add, "Mr. Thomas called Andrea, our poor secretary, early this morning and she got some friend of hers. I didn't know she knew any subs. Reba said the kids are absolutely wild. Glad I'll be back tomorrow."

Ashton says, "I'll be over in about a half hour."

I go out in the kitchen to let Mother know that Ashton is coming over.

Mother says, "Dana, I know you want to go back to work tomorrow but I'd sure feel better if you'd stay home another day. The doctor said you lost a lot of blood. Plus I'm scared of you going back to that place until the murderer is caught."

"Mom, I have to get back. I have the holiday gifts for the kids I have to get ready and I have two projects for the kids to finish for their parents. They are making booklets of their favorite stories about the holidays."

Mother asks, "Can't your sub help the kids finish those up?"

"I hope the sub does, but I can't guarantee it. Better get out of my pajamas, it's one o'clock. I'm gonna hop in the shower, Mom."

Mother offers her assistance, "Let me know if you need help. Be careful with your arm and remember we have to change the bandage when you get out of the shower."

"Luckily, it's my right arm and this is one time I'm glad I'm left handed."

The shower and getting into my jeans and sweater makes me feel a little better. As I come back into the kitchen, Mom is stirring a pot of her vegetable soup for dinner. It's my favorite comfort food and the smell of the tomatoes and spices is wonderful.

Mom stops stirring the soup and goes and gets the bandages and wrap for my arm. Even though I could probably change the dressing myself, I get a great deal of comfort from having my Mom take care of me. When you're sick, you always want your mother.

Mother asks, "Dana, what's the name of the sub in your class today?"

"Mom I'm not sure I know that. It was some name I didn't recognize so I didn't pay attention. Why are you asking?"

"My friend Martha called while you were in the shower and said that she heard that Caton's wife, Lauren, hired some friend of Andrea's to help her take care of her kids and clean out the house so she can move."

"I'm confused. What does that have to do with my sub?"

Mother continues, "Seems the woman is also a sub teacher. I wondered if it was the same person. Martha's gonna check it out."

"Guess Lauren Caton wants to get out of this town in a hurry. I can't understand it. I would think she would want to hang around until we find her husband's murderer."

Just then my cell phone rings. I run into the living room to get it before the ringing quits. Why is the cellphone never in the same room you are? Jenny is on the other end of the phone and asks how I am.

I answer, "Hey, Jenny, I'm feeling much better than last night. Can you believe this mess?"

It's good to hear Jenny's voice. I have felt so bad that Jenny was a suspect in this case. I then listen to Jenny's story as she asks for my guidance. Seems that three of my students who saw her today in a social work session have been worried because the sub was going through my files when the kids came back from lunch. The sub also made some nasty comments that she was the teacher now, and she didn't care what I had told them to do. Jenny is asking me if this is some friend of Maybelle's or Wanda's. She seems to be as vicious as them.

"What's her name, Jenny?"

I hear Jenny's answer.

I say, "Jonie Becker, I've never heard that name. Hey do you know if she is helping Lauren Caton out?

Jenny lets me know that she doesn't have that information and asks me why I asked that question.

"The sub may be a friend of Andrea's. Let me do some checking and I'll call you back."

I am furious with that woman. Who does she think she is snooping through my things and she's awfully sure of herself when she only came in for one day? You can bet I'm going to tell Thomas about it tomorrow.

As soon as I'm off the phone, I go back in the kitchen. "Mother, can you call Martha back and see if Mrs. Caton's helper is Jonie Becker?"

CHAPTER 27

The doorbell rings. Mother and I jump. Mother stops pushing the buttons on her phone. I hadn't realized how much our nerves were on edge. Mother and I aren't sure what to do. Ashton and Bud have told us to keep the doors locked and not answer.

I feel a sense of relief when I hear, "Dana, it's me. I'm gonna use my key."

As the key turns and I see Ashton's face, I must have an ashen face because Ashton says, "I didn't mean to scare you. I wanted to ring the bell to alert you before I used my key to open the door. Sorry about that."

"Mother and I are just a little jumpy. Mother's calling her friend Martha to get the lowdown on my sub. Guess this sub really stirred things up today in my class, and insulted me. The nerve. I'll be glad to get back tomorrow."

I hear Mother hang up the phone. She still uses her landline most of the time. "Well Martha says Jonie Becker is the name of Mrs. Caton's helper. Guess Andrea recommended her because she feels sorry for Mrs. Caton. Interesting that Andrea also got her to sub."

Ashton comments, "It's been a busy day at the department. With the information your secretary, Andrea, gave us we've figured out that Caton and Maybelle were skimming money from the activity fund.

I open my mouth wide, "You've got to be kidding. What were those two doing?"

Ashton explains, "Maybelle needed the money, and Caton didn't want to lose her so he was giving it to her. Looks like another arrest is coming at your school."

I question Ashton, "What do you mean?"

"We're arresting Maybelle later today. I'm on my way there now. Wanted to come by and see if you're okay."

"Oh my god, to think that Maybelle has been so busy criticizing all of us and even accused me and Jenny of the murder. That woman. I hope she never teaches. I can't believe she's a thief."

In a firm tone of voice, Ashton says, "Do not say anything to anybody. It will be public soon. Not to change the subject, can I invite myself back to supper tonight? That soup smells great." Ashton takes a whiff of the smell coming from the kitchen.

Mother, of course, loves the compliment and says, "Ashton, you always have an open invitation to dinner anytime."

"Thanks, Mrs. Lawrence. I'll be back around 6, unless something else comes up. Never did I suspect I'd be arresting school teachers."

I look at Ashton and say, "Guess we better stay off the phone for awhile so we're sure to keep our mouths shut. I'm glad you're arresting Maybelle. She gives a bad name to our profession. Ashton, when you get back I want to talk to you about the smell I remember last night. I think that might be a good clue."

"We need any clues we can get."

" See if Maybelle's wearing perfume today when you arrest her."

"Sure will. Dana, good you thought about that. Gotta go. Be safe. We still have a police car out in front. See you by six."

Ashton heads out the door after giving me a quick peck on the cheek.

It's now 4:30 and Reba is calling to check in on me.

I answer, "Hi, Reba, I'm just making a salad for dinner. How was the rest of the day?"

I'm wondering whether she has heard anything as she blurts out, "Oh my god, you won't believe what's happened. Are you sitting down?"

"What's happened now, Reba?" I ask even though I know what she is probably going to tell me.

"After school today, I stayed late and was working in my room. I heard Mr. Thomas announce that Maybelle should come to the office. Frankly I was surprised that Maybelle had stayed after school at all. I couldn't resist so I went down the hall, and saw Maybelle strut down to the office like she was some kind of queen. So typical of her."

I comment, "What else is new with Maybelle? She always thinks she's queen."

"I ran into Sara coming out of her room. Anyway we hung out in the hall but we couldn't hear anything. We waited for probably five minutes, and all of a sudden here comes Maybelle out of the office in cuffs. Can you believe it?"

I ask, "Was Maybelle saying anything?"

Reba's voice level is up, and she is talking fast, "If I could have gotten away with it, I would have taken my iPhone out of my pocket and taken a picture. What a sight it was. Ashton and the police chief were walking with her. That is the first time I have ever seen Maybelle in tears. She looked at Sara and me and smarted off to me, 'You bitch. You've caused nothing but trouble in this school. You ought to be arrested'. Then they went out the door. Can you believe the nerve of that woman?"

"I'm sorry I missed it, Reba."

"Well, that's not all. Right after Maybelle was dragged out by Ashton and the police chief, the superintendent came out with Mr. Thomas and they left. All they said was, "Good night, ladies, go on home."

"What did you do, Reba?"

Reba continues, "Sara and I went into the office to get the scoop from Andrea. Well, Andrea spilled her guts and gave us an earful. Seems that she was right that Maybelle and Caton had taken money from the student activity fund. She thinks that Maybelle killed Caton."

I ask, "I wonder whether that's the truth. It sure would be good to have this behind us and have Maybelle and Wanda gone from the school forever."

Reba says, "Andrea bets they got into a fight and Maybelle knocked him off. It would have been easy for Maybelle to put fish oil in the pie. She went on to tell us that Maybelle was always in Caton's office, with the door closed, leaving a trail of perfume behind her."

"Reba, I wonder what perfume Maybelle uses? You know it's odd that Maybelle used the term bitch to you. Remember that's what the man called me. Is it just a coincidence, or was Maybelle with some man and the man stabbed me? Maybe Maybelle got some man to do her dirty work for her?"

CHAPTER 28

"Another big scandal at Lincoln School where Principal James Caton was murdered a few weeks ago. More on the upcoming news." The local channel six news is just coming on as Ashton arrives for dinner. Mother comes out of the kitchen to hear the news.

Ashton arrives for dinner as the news is coming on, and says, "I'm glad that's over and I hope we've caught Caton's murderer."

"I can't believe you actually arrested Maybelle. I can't wait to hear all about how you proved that she was taking the student money. Is she actually spending the night in jail?"

I just finish getting the sentence out of my mouth when a picture flashes on the screen of Ashton and the chief of police escorting Maybelle into the police department.

"And now, the lead news for tonight. "Maybelle Clyde, wife of school board member Sid Clyde, was arrested tonight for theft of money from the school's student activity fund. Sid Clyde who is reported to be separated from his wife refused to comment on his wife' situation. Maybelle has been a teacher at Lincoln School for the last 10 years."

The male news commentator takes a breath. People in the community love to watch him because he is so good looking. He continues, "Maybelle's parents posted bail, and she is currently out on bond. The school board office released a statement tonight saying that the school superintendent, Jerry Schmitz, has suspended the teacher and has called for the resignation of Sid Clyde from the school board. Maybelle Clyde and James Caton, the murdered principal, were both stealing money from the fund. The question now some are raising is whether there was a quarrel over the money. Maybelle is now a prime suspect in the murder of Caton."

The female news commentator, a young blonde, continues, "In a related story, teacher Dana Lawrence was stabbed in the arm last night after Lincoln school's holiday program. She was treated and released from the city's hospital late last night. No one has been arrested for that crime. Now questions have arisen about whether Maybelle Clyde was the perpetrator."

The female commentator pauses, "Unbelievable developments at Lincoln School. Stay tuned to Channel six news for further details."

The three of us just stand there staring at the TV until Mother speaks up

"Come on and let's sit down to dinner. We all need a bowl of vegetable soup. Ashton, I made your favorite cornbread."

Ashton comments, "Oh, Mrs. Lawrence, you spoil me and I got to tell you I need to be spoiled tonight. What a day!! This soup smells so good. Do you want us not to talk about the murder during dinner?"

Mother answers. "Oh, Ashton, I'm not that rigid. I just want you to get a couple of spoons of nourishment in you, before you give us the full scoop on what happened today." Mother is dying to hear all the news.

I add, "Ashton if you don't want to tell us the gory details it's okay. I hope you'll give us the basics. As the saying goes, just the facts. Reba told us about the arrest, and how Maybelle made a snide comment."

Ashton says, "Yeah, Maybelle was pretty angry. Can you imagine how awful it would be to call your parents and ask them to post bail? She tried to tell them she was framed by Caton. I guess they believed her because they came up with the money to get her out."

I say, "I've heard that Maybelle's parents have money that they inherited from their parents."

Ashton comments, "And it looks like they will be footing the bill for her attorney. They have hired their own to represent her. I heard he isn't cheap."

I ask, "How did you really figure out she and Caton had taken the money from the account?"

Ashton answers, "That's thanks to Andrea Depper, your school secretary. Seems she had kept copies of records of the student activity fund income before she gave the accounting of funds to Caton. The student activity fund money was deposited in a checking account, and there should have been a certain amount of money in the account. Caton kept a separate accounting, and we found nine checks written to Maybelle and about five to Caton. There was over eight thousand dollars written in checks to Maybelle alone and Caton had about five thousand."

Mother says, as she throws her napkin from her lap to the table, "I can't believe that educators would actually steal from the school. They must have been really desperate."

Ashton explains further, "Lincoln School had the chili supper and the fun fest that did well financially. Caton's records showed both events only made three thousand dollars when in fact they made about sixteen thousand. Andrea knew that and had records to show it. Caton wrote the checks to himself and to Maybelle for expenses. It might have been believable but Maybelle wasn't even on the chili supper committee. Andrea submitted the actual expenses because she had receipts. Maybelle and Caton obviously had none. What stupidity!

I say, "I deliberately don't like to be on any committees that involve money. I am always afraid someone will be suspicious of how money is spent. Sure glad I wasn't on either of those committees."

Ashton continues, "Get this, at first Maybelle called the teacher's union representative to ask the union to represent her. Luckily, they told her they couldn't guarantee they could do that. She yelled at them about all she had done for them, and how could they turn their back on her. We shouldn't have allowed her two phone calls, but under the circumstances we did."

I explain, "Oh, Ashton. It's easy to understand why she called the union first. She gave them information from the school board meetings from the executive session. She pumped the information from her husband after the school board meetings. She always got preferential treatment from the union. Some of the rest of us were treated like dirt. I hope this will shake up the union, and we can clean out the current officers. Our union should be representing all of us who are trying to do our jobs."

Ashton says, "Maybelle won't be getting any more information from her husband because he had to resign from the school board. He is going to be questioned. I have to go back in tonight to question him. How did he stay with that woman as long as he did? What a fool!"

I respond, "You can't tell me that her husband didn't know she was doing some of the things she was doing. He couldn't be that stupid, could he?"

Ashton asks me, "Dana, before I go, do you remember the smell that you noticed last night. When I asked Maybelle what perfume she had on, she arched her back and said it was Angel, that was the only kind she wore."

CHAPTER 29

I say, "Ashton I think I could identify the smell from last night if I smelled it again but darn, I have never used Angel so not sure what it smells like. I'll call Reba later tonight and ask her."

I'm determined to figure out whether the culprit who stabbed me was Maybelle with her Angel perfume.

"Let me know what Reba says," Ashton comments.

Mother responds, "I'm sure no help. The only perfume I can really recognize is Shalimar and Giorgio, my favorites."

Before Ashton leaves I tell him about my horrible sub for the day, and some of the things that the social worker and Reba have told me that she did. "And here's the funny thing, she's the same person who's helping Caton's wife clean her stuff out of the house. Mrs. Caton wants to get out of town quick. I sure thought that Mrs. Caton would stay over until the murder was solved but guess not."

Ashton answers, "I thought Mrs. Caton would want to hang around too."

I say, "I think I'm going to call her tomorrow, and she how she's holding up. I feel so sorry for her, especially now that she learned that her husband stole from the activity fund. She probably really wants to leave tonight."

"Dana," Ashton says, "I know I can't talk you out of going to school tomorrow especially after the sub troubles today, but promise me you won't go anywhere other than the school and back to your condo. I'm taking both you and Reba in tomorrow and Friday. We're going to continue with surveillance and protection of you two, at least through the next couple of days. Thank heavens school will be out for your holiday break in two days."

I say, "The good thing is that Maybelle won't be at school. I'm not as frightened. I've got to get back to my condo tonight to get things cleaned up and get some things ready for class tomorrow and Friday."

Mother says, "Well, I'll stay with you tonight at your condo and maybe your brother can come over and stay with us. "How about some dessert, Ashton?"

"Good idea on both. Do stay with Dana tonight and if Bud can stay even better. We'll have a police car outside your condo building."

"I can drive Reba and me in tomorrow," I offer.

Ashton says," I got your car fixed, but you are not driving it tomorrow."

"What do you mean you got my car fixed?"

Ashton explains, "Seems that when I went to check your apartment last night, I found that all your tires had been deflated, so you wouldn't have been going anywhere. I didn't want to tell you because it was one more aggravation you didn't need,"

I open my mouth, "Oh no."

"I'm hoping Maybelle's husband can shed some light on this mess. Maybelle isn't being particularly cooperative."

I say, "While you're eating dessert, I'm going to give Reba a quick call and see if she knows the smell of Angel. I won't talk very long. I want to spend as much time with you as I can before you head back."

I press Reba's number in on my phone, "Reba, can't talk but a minute and will call you later for an update. Do you know the smell of Angel perfume?"

Reba gives me a quick no, she's sorry, but she's seen it in the star bottles.

"Thanks, Reba, call you later."

I tell Ashton and mother, "Reba says she doesn't know the smell either. Has seen the star bottles in Dillard's. Reba's a Chanel user. Wait a minute, I've got an idea."

Mother asks, "What's that?"

"After Reba and I leave school tomorrow, we can go by Dillard's and check out the smell. Oops, Ashton, you did just say you didn't want me going any place except school and home, but I can't help thinking that this Angel is important."

Ashton shakes his head up and down, "Good idea for you and Reba to check out Dillard's. I'll take you there. Maybe one of you can identify the smell. That would be an important piece of information. Here's the plan. I'm taking the two of you to school and then we'll go to Dillard's tomorrow afternoon after school."

I agree, "Sounds like a plan to me."

Ashton comments, "Now let me help clean up. This was a fantastic meal, Mrs. Lawrence, you're the greatest. You too Dana," Ashton stands up and starts collecting the dishes and takes them to the kitchen.

Mother replies, "Don't bother with that Ashton. You go find the murderer. Dana and I can clean up."

"Thanks, I'll call Bud and ask him to spend the night with you and your Mother at the condo. Bud can pick you up and I'll have the police follow you over there."

Ashton plants a kiss on my lips and whispers, "Be careful, Dana, I can't lose you."

The next morning Ashton picks Reba and me up to drive us to school. As we ride in the car to school, I ask, "How could Caton make a check out to himself? Looks like the bank would have been suspicious?" There's a light white dusting of snow on the ground and some spots of ice on the roads.

He says, "The story keeps getting worse. We looked through more records last night after interviewing Maybelle's husband. By the way, he was no help at all. Anyway, the records show that Wanda was the other person whose name was a signatory on the account so she signed Caton's checks. "

"Wanda's name was on the account too?" Reba asks.

Ashton states, "We've got to bring Wanda in again today to question her. She'll probably be arrested on this. Seems Caton, Maybelle, and Wanda were big buddies, weren't they?"

Reba says, "They were a clique. Maybelle and Wanda have been buddies for quite a while. Caton must have been so infatuated with Maybelle that he would do anything for her."

Ashton asks, "Dana, is it possible that two women attacked you Tuesday night? Could it have been Maybelle and Wanda working together?"

I frown as I say, "Two women? No. I'm pretty sure the voice I heard was a man. I know Maybelle and Wanda's voice, and it wasn't their voice."

I pause and then say, "Wait a minute, did they disguise their voice enough so I couldn't recognize it?"

CHAPTER 30

Ashton pulls in the school's parking lot, having chauffeured Reba and me to school. We are sitting in the car taking a few breaths, preparing ourselves for the day ahead. Reba and I are nervous about being at school. Ashton is apprehensive about us being here. Even with the car's heat, we all seem to be a bit frozen in time, and afraid to take the next steps to face this day.

I ask. "Ashton, just another quick question. What really happened when you interviewed Maybelle's husband?"

He replied, "Man, that was sad. He was really broken up. He just couldn't believe what Maybelle had done. He's bailed out on her. He claims he had no idea that she was taking money, He really didn't know because he paid the bills with his salary. She had her own checkbook and money that she spent only on herself."

Reba says, "Not surprising to me. She sure took him for a fool."

Ashton says, "He did say that she had a good friend at one of the banks and guess what, it is the bank where the student activity fund was held."

I just shake my head, "You have to be kidding. That Maybelle sure has friends all over the place."

Ashton adds, "We're going to be checking on the bank employee today."

I ask Ashton, "Do you really think that her husband wasn't involved? I still find that hard to believe."

"We can't really pin anything on her husband, but I have to wonder if he was that dumb about his wife." Ashton comments as he kisses me on the cheek.

"Are we still going to Dillard's perfume counter after school?" I ask.

Ashton responds, "We sure are." You two be very careful. I'll pick you up at 4 in the squad car. If we can identify the perfume, it will be a major step in the case of who stabbed you, Dana."

Reba and I get out of the car and walk into the school.

"Ms. Lawrence we're sure glad you're back," Angela one of my little students says as she enters the classroom door. She is always early for school and never eats the school breakfast. "Were you hurt bad?"

I smile at Angela and answer, "I'm happy to be back. I'm doing fine. I'm so glad to see you."

Before Angela arrived, I was going through my things. I learned that the sub had gone through a lot of my materials. She didn't put them back where she found them. Call me a little bit obsessive compulsive, but I'm very particular where everything is kept. My lesson plan book was moved to one of the drawers, and some of my other notebooks were moved. What was this sub, Jonie Becker, looking for? I wonder whether she even used my lesson plans.

Mr. Bates stops by. It's sure good to see him. When I think about all he has been through, I feel so sorry for him.

When he sees Angela, he becomes formal in his words and tone: "Miss Lawrence, can I see you in the hall?"

I come out in the hall. In a low tone of voice, he says, "Dana you should have seen your room at the end of yesterday. I had a heck of a time getting it cleaned up."

"Oh, Mr. Bates, I'm so sorry. I heard it was bad."

I feel so sad for him. This was aggravation he sure didn't need.

Mr. Bates says, "That sub you had told the kids that they didn't have to pick up anything, and they threw things all over the place. I hope she never comes back. I don't care whether she is a friend of Andrea's or not. Will you talk to your kids about their behavior?"

"Don't worry, I sure will. I can't believe it. She went through a lot of my desk drawers. Wonder what she thought she would find. I think I'll talk to Andrea and see what she knows."

"I hope you're feeling okay," Mr. Bates adds.

"I'm okay, Mr. B, can you believe everything that's happened here. How are you doing?"

Mr. B. looks sad as he speaks, "Elliott's court date has been set for March. I hope they won't be too hard on him. He made a very big mistake that ruined his career. I just hope he'll be able to teach again."

"I'm so sorry, Mr. B. I know how much Elliott means to you." I feel for Mr. B. but don't feel sorry for Elliott at all, and hope he can never teach again. He knew better than to have an affair with one of his students.

"Good morning class," I say as the rest of my students come in the room from the cafeteria where they've had their breakfast.

When the students get to their seats, I get their attention and continue, "I'm glad to be back and see all of you. I have to tell you I'm very disappointed. I understand you left quite a mess yesterday."

Devin raises his hand. I call on him. "But Miss Lawrence, Miss Becker told us that it was the custodian's job to pick up everything, and we all ought to get in trouble for not making him do his job."

Emily raises her hand, "Miss Becker said that students should do their own work, and not someone else's work."

"Boys and girls, what is our classroom rule?" I point to our posted rules and point to the one that says, Respect Property. I expect all of you to respect this classroom and keep it looking nice."

Another hand goes up. Gineen says, "Miss Becker made us do all kinds of worksheets that she brought, because she said you didn't leave any lesson plans."

By now, I am boiling mad but am careful that I don't let my students know I'm ticked off.

"We have lots of activities planned for today. I'm sorry you didn't get to do the activities I planned for yesterday. We have some fun in store today, and remember our holiday party tomorrow. For those of you who were in the holiday program on Tuesday night, I want to tell you how proud I was of each of you. You studied your parts and knew them well. You projected well on the stage."

Now Lauren's hand goes up, "I'm sorry that you were stabbed and all the air was taken out of your tires?"

"How did you know about my tires, Lauren?" I'm really confused because I didn't think that Ashton had told that information to the press.

"Why, Miss Becker told us all about it." Lauren answers.

CHAPTER 31

The Teacher's Lounge at school has become its own ghost town. No one has lunch in there. Too many bad memories of Caton's murder are housed in that room. Eventually I hope they will completely remodel it or turn it into someone's office and put the lounge elsewhere. I feel a twinge of sadness. I remember lots of good times in that lounge.

It was a small but cozy room. It probably was only about half the size of a classroom but the pale yellow walls, the fridge, and the microwave that exuded some wonderful smells of quick TV dinners made it feel like somebody's kitchen.

We solved problems, we gave each other support, we laughed about something funny one of the students said, and we complained as we all congregated around the big round table with its bright yellow cloth.

We all have our lunches in classrooms now. Sara and Reba join me in my room today. Typical of any school, there are lots of treats before the holidays. Even with all we have been through, people like Jenny Craig, our social worker, still provide goodies. Jenny won't bring in anything homemade because she's afraid because she is being accused of putting fish oil in the cherry pie.

The conference room across from the office is filled with goodies. Reba has made a quick stop there and brought a plate of cookies and fudge down to my room.

She has some news for us about Jonie Becker. "I stopped and asked Andrea about where she found Jonie Becker and how she got to sub. Andrea wasn't real happy with me. She said Jonie is a long time family friend, and is so excited to teach. Says she loved being here yesterday."

"She better never bring that woman to my class again." I am so furious about that snoopy lying woman.

Reba asks, "Isn't it interesting that she just appears as some long lost friend of Andrea's?"

I say, "Even more interesting that this same woman is helping Mrs. Caton. I'm planning on calling Mrs. Caton this afternoon to see what's going on. I want to see what's happening with her anyway. I sure thought she would want to hang around until her husband's murderer is found. Now it seems she wants to get out of here as quick as she can."

Sara says, "Come on. If you found out that your dead husband was having an affair with Maybelle and that he stole from the student activity fund, wouldn't you want to get out of town? I really feel sorry for her."

I answer, "Good point, I feel sorry for her too and want to see why she has Jonie Becker helping her."

Reba chimes in, "I'm just glad we only have a day and a half before school's out for the holiday. I need a break from all this stress, and I'm not even the one who got stabbed. Dana, you have to be ready for some time off."

"I sure am."

Reba says, "Speaking of the holidays, I wonder whether you're going to get a ring from Ashton for Christmas. He was so scared when you were hurt that it may have caused him to rethink your relationship."

I flap my hand down and say, "Oh, Reba, you're the constant matchmaker. I'm just not ready for marriage. I know, I know, don't say it. I'm not getting any younger."

Sara says, "Well I think you and Ashton make such an adorable couple. We could use some good news here."

"Sara, how long are you going to work in Wanda's class?" I ask hoping that she will spend the rest of the year here. She really is so great to work with and such a breath of fresh air after Maybelle and Wanda.

"Funny you would ask that. Mr. Thomas asked me to stay as long as I can, but as a sub I can only work so many days. Now that he learned about Maybelle, he apologized to me for conveying Maybelle's story about me"

I say, "That would be great if you could stay."

Sara continues, "Thanks, Dana. Since I have my teaching certificate he wants to hire me full time for the rest of the year. It's really tempting because I like the class. I still can't believe that Wanda ruined her teaching career, and that she and Maybelle had the audacity to try to get me fired."

"Sara, we'd love to have you here." Reba voices her pleasure.

Sara looks at both of us and says, "I told Mr. Thomas that I needed to talk with my husband and I would let him know. Working here does make my husband a little crazy. He's afraid for my safety.

I say, "I understand. I know how Ashton feels."

Sara comments, "I don't feel that scared especially since Wanda and Maybelle are gone. I think I want to do it. Got to get back to class."

The afternoon flies by with my fifth graders. I am so glad to be back. The activities I had planned with the kids went well today.

Ashton appears at my classroom door, shortly after 4:00 p.m. Reba arrived in my room just a few minutes before with her coat, hat, and gloves on. "Ladies, ready to head out for some perfume shopping? Let's solve the case of the mysterious perfume."

I have such a warm feeling when I see Ashton. Wish I could get over my fear of commitment because I really do love this guy.

Reba says. "This sure is nice having a chauffeur."

I grab my coat and my lesson plan book full of papers to be graded. Most of the people have left as we walk down the dark halls. We hear Mr. Bates in the bathroom cleaning toilets as the flushing sound echoes through the quiet hall. This place is so spooky to me after everything that has happened. The halls are dim and empty. Nobody hangs around much after school anymore because they're scared. Usually the place would be really hopping the day before the holiday break and everybody, cheery and busy. Now the halls look gray and the classroom lights are off. In the daylight I would be able to see the bright bulletin boards but dusk setting in takes any brightness away and only leaves the gloom I feel. One of my favorite places in the world has been transformed into a place of fear.

As we walk by the teachers' lounge, Aston pauses and says, "Just a minute, I want to look at something in here again." Ashton feels the tablecloth, opens the fridge, and pats the carpet on the floor around the table.

Reba and I stand out in the hall. We are not interested in going in that room. All I can see in my mind is that cherry pie sitting on the table and I think about how the dreaded pie killed Caton.

I ask, "What are you looking for, Ashton?"

"I'm just seeing if there are any traces of that fish oil, even though we looked before. I keep thinking if we could figure out what kind of fish oil it was, we could see if anyone purchased that brand. The lab called today and said they still aren't sure what kind it is but are working at it."

Reba asks, "Fish oil is fish oil, isn't it?"

I know the answer to that and say, "No, just like vitamins, there are many kinds of fish oil. I see your point, Ashton, if you could find out what kind of fish oil it is, couldn't you go to the stores and find out who bought that brand around the time Caton was poisoned?"

"Exactly, Dana, and I have to keep trying to figure that out. I asked both Maybelle and Wanda's husbands if their wives took fish oil. Maybelle's husband said never. Wanda's said she took it every day."

CHAPTER 32

As we walk out of the school, I see a squad car. In all the time we've dated, I have never ridden in a police car. In fact, in my entire lifetime, I have never been in one. Then again I have never been involved in a murder investigation.

"Ladies, your chariot awaits you." Ashton holds the front passenger door open for me and then when I am situated he holds the back seat door for Reba.

Before Ashton gets into the driver's seat, Reba says to me, "Gosh, I sure feel weird riding in the back seat of a squad car. Maybe people will think we're being arrested for Caton's murder." We both squirm around in our seats.

"I agree, Reba, it is strange."

As Ashton gets in the car, he comments, "Didn't know I would be going Christmas shopping with two great ladies. Did you have a good day?"

I reply, "I have some news for both of you. This afternoon after school, I called Mrs. Caton and had a nice chat with her. She is planning to go back home as soon as she gets things cleaned out and gets all of her husband's finances straightened out."

Ashton says, "Glad you called her. What else did you find out?"

I say, "She is so upset about learning that her husband and Maybelle were stealing from the activity fund. She says he had to be giving all the money to his mistress, Maybelle, as she called her. Mrs. Caton said he had her on a very strict budget and she barely had money to buy her kids their school clothes from Wal-Mart. She was on a roll because she told me that she hadn't had a new outfit for herself for over a year."

172

Reba says, "Well it makes sense that he was giving the money to Maybelle. She has a way of charming the pants off any man. Oops, sorry Ashton, hope I didn't offend you."

I continue, "Seems she isn't sending her kids back to school since the news broke because she is so afraid that they will be harassed. She says they are getting some horrible phone calls."

Ashton says, "I think I need to talk to her again because those phone calls might be clues to the murderer. She has to be really scared."

Reba questions me, "Did she say anything about why she hired Jonie Becker to help her clean things out? That woman is such bad news."

"That's interesting and there's some other news I have about Jonie."

"You're full of information tonight, Dana," Ashton says.

"Anyway I asked Mrs. Caton how she knew Jonie Becker. She said she found out about her from Andrea, our secretary. Andrea was so kind after her husband's death. Andrea told her that she knew somebody who would be happy to help her clean things out and take some pressure off her. She told her that Jonie would only charge her $8.00 an hour. Mrs. Caton was feeling overwhelmed so she took her up on her offer."

Ashton shakes his head, "So much for just helping out someone in need. Jonie wanted to make some money. Wow, there is quite a bit of traffic out here. Guess everyone's trying to get their Christmas shopping done after work. It's taking us a little longer to get out here than I thought it would. Sure don't like that it gets dark so early."

"Get this," I continue, "Jonie isn't working for Mrs. Caton anymore."

Reva asks, "What do you mean? Did she get all the work done?"

"I asked Mrs. Caton the same thing and she said that Jonie just told her a couple of days ago that she felt she was getting some other jobs, and would be so busy she was quitting."

Reba says, "She sure did have other jobs, didn't she? Snooping around your classroom as a supposed sub teacher."

"There's more," I add.

Ashton chimes in, "You sure did find out a lot. Good sleuthing, Dana."

I continue, "Mrs. Caton went on to say that yesterday she was going through her husband's desk and thinks some files are gone. She remembers her husband had a few files at home in his file drawers about the school and the faculty. The file drawer was not as full of files. She is angry because she thinks Jonie took the files."

Reba asks, "Didn't she see Jonie taking stuff out of the house or throwing things out?"

"Oh man, this just keeps getting worse." Ashton adds, as he calls in to the station and asks for one of the sergeants. "Hey, Chris, can you go out and take a statement from Mrs. Caton about a lady who worked for her, a Jonie Becker?"

We hear Chris say, "Sure boss, will head there now."

Ashton turns to me and says: "What else did Mrs. Caton say?'

I explain, "One afternoon Mrs. Caton needed to go to the dentist, and Jonie said she would be happy to watch the kids."

"That was a big mistake, leaving her kids with a stranger," Ashton comments as he speeds the car up to get around some blocked traffic.

"Probably, Mrs. Caton was happy for any help she could get," Reba adds.

I say, "She told Jonie that she really appreciated her thoughtfulness and left the kids with her."

Ashton comments, "I'm not sure I would have left my children with a stranger."

I say, "I agree. When Mrs. Caton was at the dentist she thought about how she shouldn't have left her kids with this strange woman. Then she thought she ought to trust somebody, and that Jonie was the school secretary's friend. She became so nervous she rushed home right after her appointment, even though she had planned some other errands. When she got home everything was fine and she felt pretty foolish."

"I would have had the same concerns and rushed home," Reba shares.

"Seems Mrs. Caton was right after all. After Jonie left, the kids said she was messing around with daddy's files. Then Mrs. Caton thought back, and realized that each day Jonie brought a large tote bag that she carried back and forth. She thinks that Jonie was looking for something in the files and just took the ones she needed."

"But why would a stranger want to take files?" Reba is confused.

"Well maybe Jonie isn't a stranger, and she is connected somehow to the murder," Ashton responds. "We sure will be checking her out. Sounds like she wanted to find some files before anyone else did. They searched

Caton's office files but didn't take a look at his home files."

I add, "Now get this. After I talked to Caton's wife, I call the Regional Superintendent of Schools to try to get some more information about this new sub, Jonie Becker."

"I'm surprised they would tell you anything about a sub," Ashton comments. He makes a right hand turn onto the street to the mall.

"I had planned to sweet talk the Superintendent's secretary but didn't have to. I told her I wanted to get an update about a sub that had been in my classroom. She asked me the name of the lady. I told her it was Jonie Becker. She asked me if the woman had another name. I said I didn't know. Was there any sub with the last name Becker? She said there is no one registered with that name."

Reba comments, "Well maybe she just registered in a different county."

"I don't think so," I respond. "I made that very comment and the secretary said in a very definitive tone that any substitute who works in the district must be registered with their office."

As Ashton pulls into the parking lot, he asks, "Why would your acting principal have a sub in the building that shouldn't be there? What's wrong with him?"

CHAPTER 33

Still in the squad car headed toward the mall, Reba shares, "It's weird that Jonie is such a troublemaker. She's a friend of Andrea's who has always seemed to be such a nice lady. Andrea's a little gossipy but she sure does her job."

I say, "I agree and she's the one who helped catch the thieves of the activity fund."

Ashton interrupts our conversation, "Hey ladies, look at the crowd at this mall. We're going to have a rough time parking. Tell you what, why don't I drop you off at the door to Dillard's and I'll go park?"

Reba comments, "Chivalry isn't dead, indeed. That's great. Thanks Ashton."

I agree and say, "I wasn't looking forward to walking in this bitter cold. I'm just glad it's not snowing."

Ashton pulls up to the door. "See you two in a few minutes."

We hop out of the car and walk very quickly into Dillard's. We wait inside the door for Ashton.

I look at Reba and say, "Reba, there must be some connection with Jonie Becker, and the murder. Why would she have been looking at Caton's file, and even take some files?"

"It really is very suspicious," Reba says.

I answer, "She sure was looking for something in my room also but what? I'm really stumped."

Ashton walks in to Dillard's shivering from the biting weather. "Brr, it's cold out there tonight, it really feels like it could snow."

I think about how handsome Ashton really is. I don't appreciate him enough. Just wish I could bring myself to make a long term commitment to him, but having gotten burned before, I am scared.

I respond, "Hey thanks, Ashton, for dropping us off. This weather makes me want to cruise to the Carribean."

"Okay, Dana, quit dreaming, we have a murder to solve," Reba pulls me back to reality.

"Let's head to the perfume counter," Ashton reminds us of tonight's mission.

I love the smell of the perfume area, and one of my favorite things to do is to spray on several different kinds of perfume to see whether I can find a new favorite.

As I am spraying on the latest Chanel, Reba says: "Dana, you're really going to smell like this perfume counter. I can't stand to try more than one on anytime I come here."

Ashton smiles at me. "I like any perfume that Dana wears, so she can try 10 of them on if she wants."

As we are chatting, a sales clerk who has the most perfectly applied make up I have ever seen approaches us. I'm not a good judge of age but I would say she is a well preserved senior citizen. Wonder how many botox treatments she's had. Her red dress on her size 4 body looks fabulous.

"May I help you find a gift or something delightful for yourself?" The clerk says to me while giving Ashton a flirty look.

Geez, I think she's old enough to be his mother or maybe his grandmother.

Ashton smiles at the clerk and then looks at me with his bedroom eyes, "Actually we are looking for Angel perfume. I want to get my wonderful girlfriend here some as a gift. Can you show me where it is?"

"Of course, you have good taste, come with me to this side of the counter. Angel is a wonderful fragrance." The clerk shows us the Angel perfume in its delightful star shaped bottle.

"Gee, I just like the bottle," Reba says.

The saleslady with her perfectly manicured hands continues her sales pitch. Her bright red nails flash. "Wait til you smell this." She sprays a bit on a small strip and hands it to me to smell. She then does the same for Reba.

After taking a whiff of it, I say, "Oh my, this is nice. I love it," I pick up the bottle and notice the price tag of $85.00. I then add, "Do you have any other products that are less expensive than Angel?" Living on a school teacher's salary and Ashton living on a police officer's pay has made me the very frugal individual I am.

Ashton comments as he takes out his credit card to pay. "I insist, Dana, nothing too good for my girl. I'll have that star bottle."

"Ashton, this is definitely the perfume," I whisper to him realizing clearly that this is the perfume I smelled the night I was stabbed in the arm.

"I thought so," Ashton then turns to the botoxed saleslady and queries, "Do you have a lot of people in this community who buy this perfume?"

"A fair amount do buy it, especially those who have excellent taste like you," our saleslady says as she flirts with Ashton.

"Well I bet my wonderful girlfriend here is the only teacher who will be wearing Angel, especially at this cost," Ashton says.

The saleslady bats her eyes at Ashton, while using her sexiest voice. "No, I wouldn't say that. There is another very sophisticated teacher who buys this perfume. I've forgotten where she works."

"Oh Ashton I think one of our teachers, Maybelle, wears this perfume," Reba adds.

"That's her name," the saleslady comments. "She comes in periodically because she uses all the Angel products. Everything that Angel has belongs to that lady. She is so particular about her appearance. "

"That's Maybelle, particular about her appearance for sure." Reba comments to the saleslady.

"Do you have any other people who have bought the perfume lately?" Ashton asks.

"Well come to think of it, there was another lady who came in on Saturday and said she was looking for the same perfume. She smelled several perfumes before she commented that she had finally found the one she wanted. She has a friend who wears it and she always loved it.

"So she didn't know the name of the perfume, only the smell?" I ask.

The saleslady answers, "That's right. I thought it was funny because she could have just asked her friend what kind of perfume it was."

"Do you happen to know the name of the lady who bought the perfume?" Ashton asks her.

The clerk answers, "That's just it. I would have if she would have used a credit card but she paid in cash, so I have the receipt but don't have her name. I was so busy that night that I didn't get her name."

"Ma'm do you remember what the lady looked like?" Ashton asks.

"Why is this so important?" The saleslady asks. "I don't want to give out too much information about my sales. I could get in trouble with the store manager."

Ashton responds as he flashes his police badge. "This is official police business and I need to know any details you can give us."

The saleslady quickly responds, "Oh my, in that case, I remember she was short—not over 5 feet, 1 and she was a bit pudgy. She had short dark hair that was beginning to turn gray. I remember thinking that she just didn't look the Angel type. That's why I remembered her."

Ashton speaks with a smile on his face. "That is very helpful. I really appreciate your help. Can you remember or can you check your sales records to see whether anyone else has bought Angel perfume?"

"Other than you, she is the only person who has bought Angel during my sales shifts. Just a minute, let me check the other sales receipts for the last week to see whether there is anyone else who bought Angel." The saleslady has become very cooperative about giving out information now that she knows its police business.

As she walks over to the other counter to go through the sales receipts, Ashton looks at me and Reba and asks, "Can you think of anyone else who fits that description?"

I comment, "That's just it, I can't think of anyone but let's keep thinking about it over dinner. Maybe it will come to either Reba or me."

The saleslady returns to the side of the counter where we are standing, "Looks like that is the only sale of Angel perfume we have had over the last week."

CHAPTER 34

We are still standing at the perfume and cosmetics counter. No more than the plastic saleslady at the counter gets her last comment out of her mouth, Ashton's cell phone rings. He walks away from the counter to take it.

Maybe there's a break in the case. So much for Ashton being off duty tonight. I bet he won't be able to join me at Reba's for dinner. This murder investigation has been so consuming, both time wise and emotionally.

Ashton comes back and says, "Ladies, are you both ready to go? We've had a change in plans."

"Hey I'm ready when you are." I figure the phone call must have yielded some critical news.

Reba adds, "No problem, I'm ready to head out. I'm getting hungry."

Ashton turns around and comments to the sales clerk, "Thanks for all your help. Have a good holiday."

As we walk away and head to the exit, I ask, "Was that a break in the case?"

We get outside the door. The brisk wind and cold temperatures that hit us in the face remind us that snow may be on the way, but we are focused on this case.

When we get in the car and get settled with our seat belts fastened, Ashton turns on the heat and says, "They've run the check I requested on the fish oil sample again and know the type it is, New Era, whatever that is. Do either of you know that brand?"

I say, "Sure, I know it. That is the best brand."

Ashton comments, "Thanks, Dana. Now the question is where is that sold and who may have purchased it. That could be an important key in the case, especially now that we have a description of who bought

Angel perfume. "I've got to get back to the station and do some work on this."

"Even if you find out which store sells that fish oil, how will you find out who may have bought it lately," Reba inquires.

I comment, "I can save you the trouble of where you can buy that fish oil because as much as I hate to admit it, that's the kind I use. You can either buy it as Whole Foods in Springfield or you can buy it at Johns Health Food store here in town. I hope I'm not a suspect again."

Ashton smiles as he says, "Dana, you're a jewel, I hardly think you are suspect anymore. I will start with the health food store here in town. I can always get a search warrant for the purchase records if I have to. Reba, sorry I can't join you and Barry tonight for dinner. I love Barry's lasagna."

Reba says, "I'm sorry too, but I understand. You need to get this case solved."

Ashton comments, "Reba, thanks for being understanding. Will you save me a doggy bag, and I'll get over there when I come back to pick Dana up?"

"You got it, Ashton, just get back as soon as you can," Reba says.

Ashton asks, "Just one more question, Dana, are you positive the Angel perfume is the smell you remember from the other night?"

I answer, "No question, Ashton, it was definitely Angel, but now we know that somebody else wears it other than Maybelle, we have to figure out who it is."

Reba adds, "Let's think about who fits the description that saleslady told us about. Dark short hair, short in height, and chubby."

I know I'm scowling as I say, "Oh my god, that description fits Jenny, but it just can't be her. She wouldn't hurt anybody." I feel like I have aged 10 years since this whole thing started."

Reba adds, "I agree with you, Dana. I refuse to believe that Jenny would do this. "Wait a minute. What if we call Jenny and ask her what perfume she wears? We can fish around for more information, including the fish oil."

"Dana, you and Reba just enjoy your evening and Barry's lasagna," Ashton reminds us nicely that he wants me to let him do his job as we pull into Reba and Barry's driveway.

"We'll save you some lasagna, get back as quick as you can." Reba answers.

Reba's husband, Barry, greets us, and gives Reba a welcome home kiss that lingers awhile. "Hey ladies, where's Ashton?"

I answer, "He has to check out a lead in the case."

Barry continues, "Lasagna will be ready in about 20 minutes."

How in love the two of them are. He is such a great guy, tall and handsome and a great cook. His blond curly hair is adorable. He really looks cute with his apron on. Reba is so lucky to have him. Barry is not only an attorney with the best law firm in town, but a great chef. How he stays thin when he cooks so well, I have never understood.

"Dana, how's your arm?" Barry asks.

I answer, "Thanks for asking, Barry, it's still very sore but better than it was yesterday. Guess it will take awhile to heal."

Barry asks, "How about a glass of wine to warm you wonderful ladies up? Can't wait to hear about today's adventures."

"Adventures is a good word for it, and where do we begin?" I say. "Ashton is sorry but guess what happened, no surprise he got called back to work. He says he'll be back, and save him some of your delicious lasagna."

"Will do, salad's made, and table's set, so we just need to wait for the lasagna. Let me pour the wine, and you ladies fill me in. I've got a fire going in the living room, so let's sit in there."

I take a seat in a chair that has an ottoman and put my feet up. Barry serves us wine. How relaxing it is to sit and take a drink.

"This fire feels so good," I say. I think about how homey Reba and Barry's place is, and so tastefully done. With Barry's salary as an attorney, they can afford many of the finer things in life. Reba is not showy, and has simple, but beautiful, taste in decorating.

As we revisit the day's events, Barry is shaking his head in disbelief. "This whole thing is like a bad dream but I have to say it's intriguing. Let's look at what we've got. Seems that the Angel perfume is critical in determining who attacked you."

Reba says, "I agree, we have to figure out who wears Angel Perfume."

Barry says, "Seems that person is very likely the same person who killed Caton. Finding out who bought the fish oil is also a very important piece of information."

"It sure is," Reba says, "I just hope it isn't Jenny Craig."

I add, "Me too, that would make me sick. Jenny sure fits the description of the person who bought Angel. We're definitely going to call her after dinner."

Barry interrupts, "Wait a minute, seems like most evidence is against Maybelle. We know she wore Angel and we know she took fish oil. Dana, do you remember anything about the man's voice you heard when you were attacked after the play? I just wonder whether it was the voice of Maybelle's husband?"

I ask, "Why would Maybelle's husband help her out in a crime?"

Barry comments, "Even with all she did, he still loved her. I bet he would cover for her."

CHAPTER 35

After we've had our delicious dinner, we continue our discussion of the murder and my attack. In response to her husband's theory that Maybelle's husband might have stabbed Dana, Reba says, "Not too likely that Maybelle's husband would help her after all the embarrassment she has caused him. Come on, he had to resign from the school board. He loved the power he had when he was there."

Barry says, "I understand your point, honey, but nothing surprises me anymore. You two know better than me how conniving and manipulative Maybelle was. She may have been able to talk him into anything. Not to change the subject, but would either of you like some tiramisu? I tried this recipe for the first time."

I ask, "Can we wait a little while? I need to let my lasagna digest. I swear, Barry, you make the best lasagna I have ever had."

My stomach is telling me it can't hold anything else, so I had better wait awhile. I am hoping Ashton gets back pretty soon.

"Good idea," Reba offers. "Why don't we have some decaf now and wait until Ashton gets back?"

Reba seems to always be able to read my mind. Guess that's what comes when you have been best buds as long as we have.

"Let me get the coffee, I have a fresh pot brewing." Barry gets up to go into the kitchen.

"Reba, I'm going to call Jenny right now. I'll just ask her some general questions about whether she's been to Dillard's lately." I pick up my phone from the table as we wait for Barry to come back with the coffee.

"Hey, Jenny, how're you doing? Can you believe we only have one day of classes left? Hey, thanks for working to get so many parents and grandparents to the holiday show on Tuesday night."

On the other end of the line, Jenny says, "I was happy to help with the holiday show. I thought it was great. Sorry I haven't told you that. I'm helping my cousin with her new boutique, and have been swamped."

I say, "Have you seen the beautiful decorations out at the mall? They're the most beautiful I've seen. Hope you've taken the time to do that."

Jenny answers, "No, I haven't. I have to do that once we're out of school for the holidays."

I continue, "Hey Jenny, I'm so excited. Ashton got me an early Christmas present. A bottle of Angel perfume. Have you ever smelled it?"

Jenny says, "No, can't say I know that fragrance. I stick with Shalimar."

I guess I have my answer about the Angel perfume. I don't think she's lying.

"Hey Jenny, I heard you may have a boyfriend. Have I missed out on something? I didn't know you were dating anybody."

On the other end of the phone, Jenny laughs, "I sure don't know about it if I do. Somebody gave you some wrong information."

I say, "Jenny, good to talk with you. See you tomorrow."

Barry comes in with our coffee. I love the smell of coffee anytime.

I say "It doesn't sound to me like Jenny's been to the mall. She says she hasn't had the time. She claims she's never smelled Angel perfume. She acted shocked when I made the comment about a possible boyfriend."

"I can't imagine its Jenny. I don't think she's a liar. I really feel sorry for her because she seems lonely, even though she's busy all the time. She doesn't have anyone significant in her life."

I say, "If she would just lose about seventy five pounds, maybe she could get some dates. She loves to eat too much."

"Come on ladies, isn't there somebody else who fits that description?" Barry asks us.

"Well I can't think of any other teachers who fit that description, and it's really bothering me," I add.

Reba says, "Me either, what are we missing?"

"Wonder whether Ashton is making any progress?" Barry asks. "Hey speaking of Ashton, why don't I give him a quick call to see how long he's gonna be."

Barry dials his cell phone. "Hey buddy, what's up? Anything I can help with, so you can come and enjoy your lasagna?" After a brief pause, Barry says, "Good news then. See you in about 20 minutes."

"Ashton said he's tracked down where the fish oil is sold. It's sold here in town, like you thought, Dana. He's there now seeing how much he can find out. They are about to close the store, so he won't be long. He figures he'll have to wait until tomorrow for them to go through records."

As we sip our coffee and think about all the clues, the doorbell rings. Barry answers the door, and it's Ashton. "Oh Barry, this house smells wonderful. I can't wait to have your lasagna."

"Sit down buddy and I'll get some for you. Just have to nuke it a few minutes."

Ashton, gives me a quick, but warm, kiss. He adds, "Hi, Reba."

We are gathered around the table and Ashton is wolfing down the lasagna and his salad.

Barry asks, "Do you think tracing the fish oil will be helpful? This could be a big break in the case, couldn't it? I hope you can solve it with that piece of evidence."

"Seems to me that if the person who purchased the fish oil fits the description of the person who bought Angel, we'll have the killer," I offer.

CHAPTER 36

We move from the table to Reba and Barry's living room for more coffee. We sit around the blazing fire that lights up the beautiful room.

"My money is on Maybelle. She uses Angel and takes New Era fish oil," Reba says.

I say, "I think Maybelle is too obvious. I think she's nasty and steals but I just don't see her as a murderer. And I know it can't be Jenny Craig. She's a warm and caring person. I just keep thinking there's something we're missing,"

Ashton says, "Let's hope we get a break in the case from Johns Health food store where the fish oil was purchased. " Ashton puts his arm around me and says, "Hey, we'd better be heading out. I need to get you home so you can get your beauty sleep."

I shake my head in agreement, "Good idea. I'm so glad to only have tomorrow left before vacation. I've got a fun day planned for the kids."

"Barry, can you drop Reba off at school tomorrow, or do you want me to come by and pick her up when I take Dana?" Ashton turns to Barry.

Barry responds, "Don't worry, I can take Reba in."

"Great, I just don't want either of them driving to school alone until this murder is solved," Ashton says.

I know he's worried. Being honest, I'm still scared from the incident Tuesday night.

Ashton says, "Hey thanks Barry, for a fantastic meal. Once we solve this mystery, I will be eager for another one."

After we get in the car and Ashton and I are in our seat belts, I say, "I need to call Mother and tell her we are on the way to pick her up."

"No need to do that. Change in plans. I called her and said she didn't need to spend the night with you. I told her I would stay and guard you." Ashton leans over and kisses me, then gives me a big smile.

"Get your eyes on the road, bad boy. Sounds like a great plan to me. Guess I won't be getting much sleep tonight."

"You've got that right."

"Oh, Ashton, you just don't know how much I'm looking forward to vacation. Sleeping in, and spending as much time with you as I can will be great. Let's hope you can get off Christmas day."

"Guess it will depend on whether I can get this murder solved. I sure hope we can be together."

As we wait for the red light, Ashton leans over and gives me a kiss, letting me know what's in store for tonight.

When the alarm goes off at 6 a.m., Ashton and I are both sound asleep. Our night of lovemaking was wonderful.

I say, "Oops, we've got 45 minutes before we have to be out the door. How about if you take your shower. I'll get the coffee on and some cereal ready. Then I'll hop in the shower when you're done."

Ashton says, "Better idea. Let's take a shower together. How about if you get the coffee on, and meet me in the shower."

While I'm starting the coffee, my cell phone rings. I answer expecting it to be Reba.

A deep voice comes on the line, "Just because you've got that cop as a boyfriend and live in, don't think you're safe. I'm gonna get you." I hear the click sound, and am stunned and shaking. I thought I was safe with

Ashton here with me. I run into the bathroom yelling, "Ashton."

Ashton turns off the shower, opens the shower door, sees me shaking, and says, "What's happened?"

"I just got a threatening call on my cell, " I answer.

Ashton grabs my phone as I'm telling him what was said. He says, "Damm, unknown. I should have figured the person wouldn't give us a clue."

"Can you trace the call?" How did they get my cellphone number? I ask Ashton.

"Dana, there's no way to trace this call and sounds like the caller is watching the condo. Calm down and take a deep breath."

I start crying, "Ashton, will this never end? I'm so scared."

"Shh, I know. I'm so sorry. Don't worry, we'll figure this out. I had a police officer in a car on the street, so let me call, and see if he saw anything unusual. Was it a male voice?"

"Yes, it was definitely a male voice."

I am pacing while Ashton is on the phone to the officer. After he hangs up, he says, "He said he didn't notice anything unusual at all. Lots of cars passed by but none even slowed down. Anybody could have seen my car pull in to your garage."

I say, "But the garage is shut so they would have had to follow us last night."

Ashton says, "Someone had to see me pull my car in your garage. No car seemed to be behind me."

Ashton pauses and keeps thinking, "There were a few cars parked on the street but nothing looked unusual."

"Someone had to have followed us, Ashton, or else they were just guessing that you and I were together last night. Remember you took me to school and picked me up at school. Come to think of it, it could be someone from school who knew that information but who?"

CHAPTER 37

Ashton drives me to school. He is holding my one hand while he drives. Both of us keep looking out the mirror to see if someone is following us. We are both quiet while we try to think about who could have made the threatening phone call.

I break our silence as we pull up at school. "Ashton, it makes sense to me that someone's following us, but I sure don't see another car. My gut feeling says it has to be someone here at school, but who?"

Ashton answers, "Dana, you're right, and it scares the hell out of me that you are going to be at this school. I'm going to order even more security today. I'll put a couple of plain clothes officers out and in. They're going to be hanging out close to your classroom and outside."

I say, "Thanks, Ashton, I'm sure I'll be okay." Wish I was as sure of that as I am saying I am.

Ashton gives me a big hug. "It's gonna be okay, Dana, I'm not going to let anything happen to you."

"I'm so lucky I have you." I give Ashton a kiss.

"I have to get the fish oil records from the store today. Then I'll be discreetly hanging out. We've got to be getting too close for the murderer. I'm thinking it has to be someone either at the school or someone who is related to somebody at school. Have a good day and remember this is the last day before your vacation."

The intercom buzzes about 10 minutes after I have arrived. I'm getting my lessons organized for the day.

Mr. Thomas, our acting principal, announces, "Good morning staff, I hope all of you have a great last day before our holiday break. I want to thank each of you for all you have done during this difficult time. I need to remind you that from eleven thirty until twelve forty five

Mrs. Depper and I have the secretary appreciation luncheon. If you have an emergency during that time, you can call us at the central office. I wish all of you a great day."

Mr. Thomas has worked hard to keep everyone calm and on task during this difficult time. I hope he stays and finishes out the year.

I am always overwhelmed by the wonderful gifts I receive from my students and families. The gifts that come in this morning, as I greet my students the last time before our holiday break, truly put me back in the holiday spirit. So many parents have written notes that they appreciate all I've done. Those thank you's are worth any teacher's salary. Just knowing that you are appreciated by your students and their parents makes all the long hours worthwhile. Today they help me forget my current troubles.

This afternoon I am looking forward to giving my students the gifts I have made for them. I have created an album with their pictures and their best work in it. I managed to learn enough about scrapbooking to do this project. I am pleased with what I've done, and think the children will be also.

It is mid-morning and my students are working on a holiday math project using red and green M&Ms. I love to use manipulatives for math. I find that, even with fifth graders, manipulatives, especially food, really motivate them and make math fun.

I am walking around the room giving the kids encouragement; when I overhear one of my students, Betsy, make a comment about another staff member looking like Jenny Craig.

When Betsy looks up at me, she says, "Miss Lawrence, you look surprised. Is everything okay?"

A light bulb clicks in my head. Why hadn't I thought of that person before? Is it really possible? It does make sense. Why didn't I think about the murderer meeting the description that the perfume counter clerk gave of the person who bought Angel. I don't think I have forgotten anything. I am excited that I have solved the mystery. I'm also frightened the murderer is here at school today. An hour until lunch and I can hardly contain myself. I know what I need to do and will need Reba's help. I know who killed Caton, and just need some more evidence to prove it.

I answer Betsy, "Everything's fine, Betsy, you are really observant. I guess those M&Ms fuel your brain."

The rest of the morning creeps by. I am eager to carry out my plan.

As soon as we have our lunch break, I find Reba. I whisper what I've discovered.

Reba says in a low tone of voice, "Oh my goodness, Dana, you're brilliant, why didn't we think of that earlier? The killer is right here and we didn't see the clues before. Wonder what the motive was?"

"Well, here's what we're going to do. I'm going to go through the desk and you are going to stand in the hall and watch for anyone who might come by. If I find anything, I'm going to call Ashton right away and tell him to come over. I'm hoping I will find at least one shred of evidence."

We head down to the location of the killer. No one is in that room now. I look out the window, and see a police car stationed across the street. I sit down at the desk and am prepared. If anybody goes by and wants to know what I'm doing, I'll say I was checking on some copies I requested.

Reba says, "Don't take too long, Dana, somebody could come down the hall any minute."

"I know, I'm nervous. Tell me right away if you see anyone."

I start looking through the middle drawer. It's very neat. Not much is in there, but pens, pencils, and a few keys. I open the top left hand drawer and nothing unusual is there. When I get to the bottom left hand drawer I see several files. I'm trying to move through things as quick as possible before anybody comes in. Stuck under the files is a receipt for Angel perfume. Got the evidence.

CHAPTER 38

The evidence with the perfume receipt should be enough to show who my attacker really was. Now it all makes sense to me. I call Ashton's cell phone right away but get his recording. What am I going to do now?

"Reba sticks her head in the door. "Mr. Bates is coming down the hall with the mop. What should I do?"

I hear the sound of the mop swishing back and forth as Mr. Bates gets closer. It makes me cringe. I am so nervous.

"We don't need to worry about Mr. Bates. Tell him I'm looking for a form."

"Okay, Dana, but hurry, this scares me."

I say, "I've got what I need. Don't worry."

My hands are sweating. I call Ashton again, but get his answering machine. I leave a message to come to school right away and tell him it's an emergency. Hope he gets here soon.

We only have 20 minutes more until we have to get back to class. I look out the window and see Mr. Thomas and Andrea pulling in the parking lot.

I say, "Reba, they're out of the car and headed for the door. We're going to have to confront them ourselves."

Reba answers, "How are we going to do that? Dana, I'm scared."

I'm shaking, but I know what I have to do. I've got to get myself back in control. I have to remain nonchalant and calm. It sure is hot in here.

"Are you sure we shouldn't wait for Ashton, what if we get hurt?" Reba has a look of fear on her face. She is pacing up and down the hall.

I say, "Reba, pull it together. We have to act like

nothing's wrong when they come in."

Just then my phone rings. Ashton's voice says, "Dana, go to your classroom right away. When the kids come back, lock yourself in."

I answer, "I can't do that. I'm in the office now. I gotta go. Come to the school office right now. I need you."

I hang up the phone just as Andrea and Mr. Thomas walk in.

Andrea looks at me and Reba, who has now come inside the office. "What do you ladies need? We had such a nice luncheon, didn't we?" She looks over at Mr. Thomas and smiles.

Mr. Thomas responds, "We sure did. Is there something we can help you with? I know you're probably in a hurry since your class will be back in about 10 minutes." He seems clueless.

I say in a quiet voice, "Oh we need a lot, Mr. Thomas. A lot of explanation from Andrea here. Andrea, why don't you tell Mr. Thomas about Angel perfume and fish oil?"

Mr. Thomas says, "Ladies quit the silly talk. I order you to go back to your rooms right away."

Andrea smiles at Reba and me and says, "Ladies, I know you're under a lot of stress with all that's going on. Maybe we can spend some time together after school today."

Mr. Thomas says in a definitive tone, "That's a good idea, Andrea, now let's all get back to work."

He is in for a shock. He is soon to find out that he isn't really the authority he thinks he is.

I get up my courage. I stand tall and look Mr. Thomas in the eye. I have come too far not to continue, "Not before I tell you that our school secretary knows all about the murder of Mr. Caton."

I turn to Andrea with a frown on my face, "Why did you do it, Andrea? Why did you hate Caton so much?"

"Mr. Thomas, please tell these ladies to stop this ridiculous talk. I have work to do, and ladies, you do too? Excuse me I have to get to my desk."

As Andrea walks to her desk, Ashton walks in the door with another officer, "Andrea Depper, you are under arrest for the murder of James Caton and the attempted attack on Dana Lawrence." Ashton reads Andrea her rights.

Mr. Thomas's face turns the color of paste. He has his mouth open, "What is happening here?"

Ashton looks at him, "I'm sorry to tell you. There is strong evidence that Mrs. Depper poisoned Mr. Caton and also, together with her husband, stabbed Dana."

Andrea's face is lipstick red as she says, "This is absolutely ridiculous. I'll have your job." She looks viciously at Ashton and then at me, "and yours too, miss smarty pants. This is all a big mistake, Mr. Thomas, I can assure you I'm innocent. I'll be cleared and this two bit police department is going to be sued for accusing me falsely."

"Let's go, Mrs. Depper, your husband will be joining you at the police department." Ashton and his colleague lead Andrea out. They wait to cuff her until they are outside the building. They want to make sure that no children see this scene.

Reba and I are left in the office with Mr. Thomas. Reba looks at me and says, "Dana, good for you, figuring this whole thing out."

Reba then turns to look at Mr. Thomas and says,

"I guess you're lucky Andrea didn't poison you. Come to think of it, I sure hope she didn't have any poison with her when she went to the luncheon today."

Mr. Thomas answers, "I know you are very upset over this. I'm so sorry. I don't know what to say, Dana, will you be okay to go back to class?"

He doesn't address Reba, but he should have known she was going to make an unflattering comment to her after he was so flippant with us.

I say, "I'll be fine. I'm so relieved this whole mess is over. Reba, let's get back to our kids. We only have a couple of hours left before break. Thank goodness."

I feel such a sense of relief when I go back to class. We have a great time at our holiday party. I'm glad the kids don't know anything right now. They can hear the news directly from their parents. The time over break will give all of us a chance to forget about what a chaotic first semester this has been. We all need a chance to regroup and get rejuvenated.

What awaits us next semester?

CHAPTER 39

"I want to propose a toast to Ashton for his hard detective work in bringing justice to the staff at Lincoln School." My brother Bud has his champagne glass raised as we prepare to be seated for our Christmas dinner at my Mom's house.

"Here, here," my Mother says as we all raise our glasses and cheer. My nephew is excited to toast, even if it is with grape juice.

Ashton says, "Just a minute. I want to propose a toast to my beautiful Dana who has survived this last month, and who figured out who Caton's murderer was."

"You guys are a good team," Shelley, the ever present matchmaker, says.

The subject is dropped as we all dig into the turkey and dressing, and mashed potatoes, and on and on. We have decided to enjoy our wonderful dinner before coming back to the topic of all that has happened at my school.

After stuffing ourselves and then cleaning up, we gather around the fireplace in Mother's family room. It has been a great day with just a light dusting of snow, adding a calming picture of the world outside. The warmth of the fireplace feels so good. My hands are tingling with the feel of the fire.

"Are you looking forward to going back to school now that this mess is over, Dana?" Bud asks.

I answer, "I really need this break, but I'll be eager to get back to my kids, and the many good people that I work with at Lincoln.

Shelley, my sister in law, says, "Dana, you deserve a break after all you've been through."

I say, "Every time I think about how Wanda and

Maybelle thought they were the school queens, I get upset. To think that they tried to pin Caton's murder on me, and Jenny Craig, our social worker. It gives me great pleasure to know they'll never teach again. I guess sometimes justice does prevail."

Mother asks, "Ashton, I heard that Andrea and her husband had a previous charge of attempted murder, but why did Andrea want to kill Caton? Was he that bad of a boss?"

Ashton answers, "Caton was blackmailing the Deppers. They were originally charged with attempted murder."

Bud asks, "Blackmailing? What did Caton think he was doing?"

Ashton says, "The Deppers tried to poison their landlord a few years ago in New York. The guy didn't die, but it went to trial and a mistrial was declared. They got off. Turns out that Caton found out about it from a friend, and he blackmailed them. Said if Andrea refused to follow any of his orders he would tell everybody what they had done, and he would make sure she never got another job."

Shelley says, "Wonder if Andrea poisoned her landlord with fish oil?"

Ashton replies, "We may never know that. Obviously her mode of operation for murder is poison."

Mother says, "Caton was a jerk, I'm not condoning what the Deppers did, but he just never stopped doing mean things."

Bud says, "Don't forget that old man Depper is the one who stabbed our Dana. How did you figure that out, Ashton?"

Ashton adds more information, "Andrea was there, but Depper stabbed Dana because he had arm strength that Andrea didn't have.

Shelley asks, "Did Andrea turn on her husband, and give you that information?"

Ashton says, "Andrea didn't rat on him. Our other officers found the knife in their house when we got a search warrant. It still had his fingerprints on it. Why he was so stupid that he didn't get rid of the knife, we'll never know."

I say, "I really think the Deppers thought they would never get caught."

Shelley questions, "What was the deal with that terrible sub that Dana had? Wasn't her name Jonie something?

Ashton says, "Another interesting fact. Jonie Becker was Mr. Depper's sister. They had her ingratiate herself with Mrs. Caton. When she was supposedly helping Mrs. Caton, she was really make sure that Caton had no files around the house about the Depper family."

I add, "Then Andrea had her pose as a teacher, and she only has a high school diploma. She came to my room to do some more snooping."

Ashton says, "I have to hand it to Dana. She did figure out that it was Andrea. It scares the hell out of me to think that Dana was working in the building with a murderer."

Bud looks at me as he asks the question, "What's going to happen now in the school system, Dana?"

I know it also scared Bud to think that I was working in the building with a murderer.

I answer, "Mr. Thomas called me a couple of days ago to make sure I was okay. I got some information from him. Sara is going to sub the rest of the year in Wanda's room. They will be interviewing a December graduate to fill Maybelle's position. They're going to transfer one of the central service secretaries over to our school. Mr. Thomas, our principal, will finish the year out."

Mother speaks up, "Ashton, what will happen to all these terrible people? I sure hope all of them go to jail for a long time."

Ashton looks over at Mother as he answers, "You and me both, Mrs. Lawrence. Andrea and Carl Depper are in jail awaiting trial. Their bail was set so high they couldn't make it. In jail they sit. Andrea actually poisoned Caton, but we know that Mr. Depper is the one who stabbed our Dana."

"I'd like to bust that guy's jaw myself." Bud has a disgusted look on his face.

Ashton answers, "I would too, Bud, he certainly won't get the time that Andrea will, but he'll get some. Just think there is going to be a lot of excitement in this community over the next several months with Wanda and Maybelle's trial. Don't forget about Elliott Bates who molested his student. His trial will start in January, "

"What else could possibly happen? We don't need any more trouble," Shelley says. "It's nice just to be able to sit here and enjoy some peace and quiet."

Just then, Ashton's cell rings. He walks out of the room to take the call.

"Oh no, not today, "I comment.

Ashton walks back in the room. "Thanks for the great dinner and relaxing day. I loved it. I've gotta go. Another case just came in."